That Smell & Notes from Prison

That Smell

&

Notes from Prison

Sonallah Ibrahim

Edited and translated
by Robyn Creswell

A NEW DIRECTIONS BOOK

The translator would like to acknowledge the generous support
of the Dorothy and Lewis B. Cullman Center for Scholars and Writers
at the New York Public Library.

Manufactured in the United States of America
New Directions Books are printed on acid-free paper.
First published as a New Directions Paperback (NDP1248) in 2013
Published simultaneously in Canada by Penguin Books Canada Limited

Library of Congress Cataloging-in-Publication Data
Ibrahim, Sun'Allah.
[Tilka al-ra'ihah. English]
That Smell and Notes From Prison / Sonallah Ibrahim;
edited and translated by Robyn Creswell.
p. cm.
Includes bibliographical references.
ISBN 978-0-8112-2036-1 (paperbook : alk. paper) —
ISBN 978-0-8112-2062-0 (ebook)
1. Political prisoners—Egypt—Fiction. 2. Political fiction. I. Creswell, Robyn.
II. Ibrahim, Sun' Allah. Yawmiyat al-wahat. English. Selections. III. Title.
IV. Title: Notes from prison. V. Title: That Smell and Notes From Prison.
PJ7838.B7173T513 2013
892.7'36—dc23
2012032484

1 3 5 7 9 10 8 6 4 2

New Directions Books are published for James Laughlin
by New Directions Publishing Corporation
80 Eighth Avenue, New York, NY 10011

Contents

Translator's Introduction

Sonallah Ibrahim's first book, *That Smell*, was published in Cairo in 1966. The print run was quickly confiscated, though not before a few copies were passed on to local critics, who were almost as unwelcoming as the censors. Yahya Haqqi, one of the grand old men of Egyptian letters and one of Ibrahim's early mentors, wrote that he was "nauseated" by the novel, lamenting "its lack of sensibility, its lowness, its vulgarity." Illegal and abbreviated editions subsequently appeared in Egypt and abroad, but it was only in 1986 that a complete edition was published in Cairo. By that time, Ibrahim had become an established novelist and *That Smell* was recognized, especially by young writers, as a watershed in Arabic literature—a work of sly sophistication and prescient critique, a fiction to frighten the status quo.

It is not obvious, especially to foreign readers at a distance of almost fifty years, why this short work provoked such a violent response. The reaction of the authorities, which Ibrahim recounts with exasperated amusement in his introduction to the 1986 edition (translated here as an afterword), focused on the novel's representation of sexual matters. But these scenes, which are brief and rather chaste, do not explain such hostility. In fact, there is little in the story that strikes one as explicitly subversive. It begins with an unnamed narrator being released from prison, followed by scenes of his visits to family and friends while re-familiarizing himself with Cairo, his native city. At night he signs a register of house arrest brought to his door by a policeman. The human setting, as with much of Ibrahim's fiction, is lower-middle-class: government clerks, newspapermen, low-ranking army officers. There is not much plot in the conventional sense and the narrator's tone is remarkably blank. He makes no attempt to set his story within a larger historical context, nor does he pass judgment on the things he sees and hears. The story's central drama, such as it is, revolves around his sporadic attempts to write, though what he is trying to compose is never clear (a novel, a poem, a letter?). Even in this case, not much happens. Confronted by an empty page, he usually ends up smoking or masturbating or spying on his neighbors rather than writing.

That Smell is essentially a roman à clef. When he wrote the novel in his late twenties, Ibrahim himself had just been released from prison. He was arrested for political conspiracy in 1959, along with most other Egyptian Communists, during a round-up ordered by the president, Gamal Abdel Nasser, who had came to power in a military coup in 1952. Ibrahim was given a seven-year sentence of hard labor and ended up serving five, most of them in al-Wahat prison camp in Egypt's Western Desert. Conditions in the jail were harsh. Prisoners were tortured, several were beaten to death. The narrator of *That Smell* has also been a political prisoner, though this is implied rather than stated. In one of the opening scenes, he spends the night in a holding pen before being released back onto the streets (another autobiographical detail). A fellow inmate asks what he is in for—drugs? robbery? counterfeiting?—only to be met with a series of denials. Here, as elsewhere in the novel, politics is what cannot be mentioned, or what no one will talk about except indirectly. This unspoken taboo extends to the narrator, who never gives his opinion about life under the military regime, or its treatment of political opponents. Ibrahim's writing style is a kind of corollary to this. It is a style defined by all the things it leaves out: metaphors, adjectives, authorial commentary. His narrator has the impassivity of a trauma victim: he sees and hears and reports, but makes no claim to understand. This minimalism shocked contemporary Arabic readers. Many found Ibrahim's style more disquieting than the story's themes or content. Even now it is not easy to see how he arrived at this way of writing, which breaks so violently with the norms of literary Arabic.

Ibrahim's experience as a Communist is central to his novel. One might even understand his later career as a writer as an attempt to remain faithful to the history of that movement, long after the Egyptian party ceased to exist. In an autobiographical essay about his years as a militant, Ibrahim claims that when he became a Communist in 1954 it was in part for literary reasons. As a young reader, he had a passion for *policiers* and historical swashbucklers—*Robin Hood, The Three Musketeers, Captain Blood,* and the stories of Arsène Lupin. (Traces of this passion for the pulps are still evident in the overheated fantasies of *That Smell,* as well as the appearance of the radio show, "The Shadow," in the closing sequence.) By the time he was seventeen, Ibrahim was involved in clandestine political work for Haditu, an acronym for the Democratic Movement for National Liberation, one faction in Egypt's patchwork of Marxist movements. "There is no doubt," Ibrahim writes, "that my commitment to clandestine activities stemmed from the adventure stories I loved so much," stories that had also taught him the virtues of "sincerity, loyalty, self-sacrifice, asceticism, and chivalry."

The ups and downs of the Egyptian Communist party are notoriously difficult to track. This volatility is partly due to factionalism and partly to the movement's shifting attitudes toward President Nasser. The party was always small and there were almost as many intellectuals as workers. When the first cells and study groups were founded in the 1930s, the party was mostly led by well-to-do Egyptian Jews. These were committed internationalists and anti-fascists, wary of the chauvinism they perceived in Egypt's Islamist and nationalist parties. (The early prominence of Jews in many Arab Communist parties would compromise recruitment efforts, especially after the establishment of Israel in 1948.) The Communists initially welcomed the coup of 1952, which put an end to the monarchy of Farouk and, soon after, the British occupation of Egypt. But the honeymoon was short. Twenty days after seizing power, the ruling clique violently suppressed a strike by textile workers and executed two labor leaders. Among the leftists, rumors began to circulate that the CIA had had a role in the takeover. The next four years were characterized by tensions between the Communists and Nasser, as well as between different factions within the movement, whose activists disagreed over whether or not to support the new regime. When Ibrahim joined Haditu in 1954, it was among those factions that enthusiastically backed the officers.

In the aftermath of the Suez War of 1956, having faced down

Britain, France, and Israel, Nasser was at the height of his powers. He was a popular leader in the movements for anti-colonialism and pan-Arabism, and he soon emerged, along with Tito and Nehru, as a driving force in the Non-Aligned Movement. Egyptian Communists had little choice except to get behind him. But the regime never returned these friendly feelings. In 1958, a coup by Iraqi officers seemed to signal that country's turn toward communism and away from pan-Arabism, and Nasser began to worry about his domestic reds. This was the proximate cause for the arrests of 1959, in which Ibrahim was caught up. The consistent support his faction had given Nasser ended up counting for nothing.

One irony of this story is that it was during the years of Ibrahim's imprisonment, in the early 1960s, that Egypt turned decisively toward the Soviet Union in foreign policy and toward socialism on the domestic front, with ambitious programs of nationalizations and land reform. Cultural relations also became closer. Many Egyptian intellectuals made the trip to Moscow—Ibrahim spent a year there in the early seventies studying film—and Cairo's literary journals were full of the news from the USSR, in particular the rise of liberal-minded poets such Yevgeny Yevtushenko and Andrei Voznesensky. This new closeness between Nasser and the Soviets led to a number of surreal instances in which Egyptian Communists publicly and voluntarily expressed their support for a regime that had jailed and tortured them. A further irony is that Ibrahim and many others were granted an early release from prison in 1964 only because of Khrushchev's visit to celebrate the construction of the Aswan Dam, designed and financed by the USSR. The Soviets noted that the Premier could hardly make Nasser a Hero of the Soviet Union when Egyptian jails were full of Communists. Less than a year later, the two largest Communist parties in Egypt met and voted to dissolve themselves, instructing their memberships to enroll in Nasser's newly formed Arab Socialist Union. They hoped to have some influence on the regime's policies by shaping them from the inside, but this was not to be. As Joel Beinin, a historian of the Arab left, has written, "The Egyptian communists were caught up by their embrace of the national movement and ultimately destroyed by it."

This convoluted history of alliance, enmity, and cooptation is the prelude to *That Smell*. The narrator's stupor is the daze of depoliticization, a sense that the large battles have already been fought and lost. In his meetings with friends and family, the talk is mostly about marriage, the newest American appliances, and how to get ahead in the new bureaucracies. *That Smell* is a political novel in the sense that it evokes, from the inside, the feeling of life *after* politics. It registers the cooling temperatures and lowered expectations of a moment when Nasser's "holy march" toward Arab unity has stalled in the sands of economic reality and popular disaffection.

The most pervasive symptom of this stagnation, in Ibrahim's fiction, is sexual. The narrator of *That Smell* is a prototype for the heroes of his later novels: a bookish loner whose encounters with women, real or imagined, are awkward and anticlimactic. His one meeting with a prostitute turns into a comedy of errors. It is the narrator's sexual powerlessness that seems to have most worried the Egyptian censors. In his

1986 introduction, Ibrahim writes of being interrogated by an officer in the Ministry of Information shortly after the novel was printed. Why does the hero refuse to sleep with the prostitute, the official wants to know? Can't he get it up? The censors were presumably more comfortable with the virile heroes of socialist realism—the dominant form for the novel in Egypt at the time—who were forever building dams, making speeches, and machine-gunning the Zionists. But it is Ibrahim's novel that was more attuned to its times. It is now often seen as a work that foreshadowed the humiliation of the 1967 War, a novel that told the truth about Egyptian impotence even as the regime trumpeted its fictions of victory.

I've noted that there is a little mystery about how Ibrahim arrived at the style of his first work, a style that is at once simple and strange, or strange because it seems so simple. Compared to Egyptian writers of the previous generation—Naguib Mahfouz, Tawfik al-Hakim, Taha Hussein—Ibrahim's prose is very plain. The syntax is straightforward and even monotonous (a monotony that is meant in part to mimic the dreary routines of the narrator's life under house arrest). There are no spiraling clauses and only the most basic transitions, usually "and" or "then." There are no ten-dollar words, only everyday nouns and verbs. It is a style that is aggressively unliterary. Reading it, one feels Ibrahim forcing the native eloquence of Arabic prose to make room for a degree of inelegance and even ugliness. This inelegance, so disturbing to the novel's original readers, is one of the elements I find lacking in the previous English translation, *The Smell of it & other stories* (1971), by Denys

Johnson-Davies. In that edition, Ibrahim's lower-middle-class characters speak a plummy version of English and the unbroken block of the original Arabic text—a layout that fits the stream-of-consciousness narrative—is transformed into tidy paragraphs and indented dialogue.

For some hints about how he arrived at this intentionally unstylish style of writing, and also for some sense of Ibrahim's life in prison, we can turn to the *Yawmiyat al-Wahat*, translated here as *Notes from Prison*. This is a series of journal entries Ibrahim wrote during his last two years in prison, from the spring of 1962 to the spring of 1964. In November 1963, Ibrahim transferred the contents of these secret notebooks to Turkish Bafra-brand cigarette papers, to make them easier to smuggle out. Excerpts from this archive first appeared in the Cairene magazine *al-Hilal* in 2003. The full diary, with accompanying notes and an introduction by Ibrahim, was published the following year. He summarized its contents in this way: "Writing and its difficulties, the role of the writer and his formation, the many contradictory theories of the novel—these considerations take up a large portion of my notebooks." In the earlier entries Ibrahim dreams of a heroic writer who will "dive into the depths of the people" and "reveal the way forward"; later entries are increasingly concerned with questions of technique and style. The Arabic version runs to well over a hundred pages. For the purposes of this translation, I have selected only a small portion, about one fifth of the total. Many of the notes concern writing projects that never came to fruition, or would require context beyond the scope of this edition. I have focused instead on those entries I take to be relevant to the composition of *That Smell*. Read in this way, as prolegomena to the novel, they offer a fascinating glimpse into Ibrahim's procedures as a reader and a writer.

"Prison was my university," Ibrahim writes in his own introduction to the *Notes*, and indeed the entries read at times like a syllabus, or a wish list for future reading. "Must read *Ulysses*," he writes in December 1962, when he was twenty-five years old. And three months later, "Must read Proust." The diaries have relatively little to say about prison routine or with Ibrahim's personal life, in part because he feared the notes might be seized and used against him. Nevertheless, a picture does emerge between the lines of an intensely intellectual environment. Most of the Communists' reading seems to have been acquired through the prison guards, who occasionally spent a week in Cairo or Alexandria and were easily bribed. Cultural supplements from Cairene newspapers formed a large part of the prisoners' reading. An ex-leader of the party, Henri Curiel, who arranged for the prisoners' legal defense from his exile in Paris, also sent copies of *La Nouvelle Critique*, which one of the French-speaking inmates would translate for the rest. The arrival of Naguib Mahfouz's *The Cairo Trilogy* caused such excitement that the prisoners drew up a waiting list for readers. During the day, the inmates buried their library in the sand outside the cells. (This same bookish and clandestine milieu was cultivated by Muslim Brotherhood prisoners, who shared jails with the Communists, though the two groups kept mostly to themselves. Indeed, much of modern Egyptian intellectual history was born in Nasser's prisons.)

Three central interests stand out in Ibrahim's diaries. The

first is the importance of literature from the USSR. Soviet culture was viewed by the Egyptian Communists as a mirror, a model, and a warning. It was more advanced, but also more damaged than their own. The diary is full of the news about *Novy Mir*, the Soviet monthly that briefly served as a forum for liberal opposition in the wake of de-Stalinization. For fathomable reasons, one of the first books Ibrahim read after his release is Solzhenitsyn's *One Day in the Life of Ivan Denisovich*, first published in *Novy Mir* in 1962. There are several entries that hint at connections Ibrahim was making between Soviet and Egyptian experience, often by way of citation rather than commentary. In May of 1963, he reproduces a passage by Yevgeny Yevtushenko, among the most famous poets in the world at the time (now hardly read), whose memoirs were being serialized in the French magazine *L'Express*: "To explain away the cult of Stalin's personality by saying that it was imposed by force is, to say the least, rather naïve," Yevtushenko writes. "Many genuine Bolsheviks arrested at that time refused to believe that this had happened with his knowledge, still less on his personal instructions. Some of them, after being tortured, traced the words 'Long Live Stalin' in their own blood on the walls of their prison." Given what Ibrahim says elsewhere about the Egyptian Communists' perverse relation to Nasser, which he describes as "absolute support from our side; repression and murder from his side," it is easy to see why this particular anecdote jumped out at him.

Ibrahim's dilemma might be thought of in this way: how to write oppositional art when the regime in power has already stolen your best lines? The attractiveness of Yevtushenko, it would seem, is that he briefly supplied a model for how one might remain a Communist despite communism—or, as he writes in his memoir, how one maintains "faith in the original purity of the revolutionary idea despite all the filth that has since desecrated it." It is from the Soviet writers that Ibrahim gets his obsession with "telling the truth," an idea that crops up incessantly in the writings of Yevtushenko and others quoted in the *Notes*. For the Soviets, this meant telling the truth about Stalin and the Gulag. For Ibrahim, it meant telling the truth about Nasserism.

But what is the style of truth telling? Here is where the second, somewhat more surprising feature of these diaries appears, their immersion in American literature and especially in Hemingway. A long series of notes from June 1963 concern Carlos Baker's book, *Hemingway, the Writer as Artist*, which had been recently translated into Arabic by the Palestinian scholar Ihsan Abbas. Ibrahim's notes focus on *The Green Hills of Africa*, Hemingway's 1935 account of a hunting trip on the Serengeti Plain. Ibrahim quotes from Baker's citation of a long discussion between Hemingway and Pop, another hunter, where they discuss what it's like to witness a revolution. The conversation also serves as a statement of literary method. Hemingway as himself says about revolutions,

> It's very hard to get anything true on anything you haven't seen yourself because the ones that fail have such a bad press and the winners always lie so. Then you can only really follow anything in places where you speak the language. That limits you of course. That's why I would never go to Russia. When you can't overhear it's no good. All you get are handouts and

sight-seeing. Any one who knows a foreign language in any country is damned liable to lie to you…. If I ever write anything about this, it will just be landscape painting until I know something about it. Your first seeing of a country is a very valuable one. Probably more valuable to yourself than to any one else, is the hell of it. But you ought to always write it to try to get it stated. No matter what you do with it.

You ought to always write it to try to get it stated. The phrase is underlined in Ibrahim's diary. The Arabic translation reads, "*Uktub, uthbit ma tarahu wa-ma tasma'uhu*": "Write, set down what you see and hear." It is clear that Ibrahim's minimalism owes something to Hemingway, a fact I have tried to keep in mind in my own translation. Might this iconic, endlessly imitated style come back to English readers, made strange and new after a detour through Cairo? Ibrahim takes other tips from Hemingway. The technique of italicized flashback, used several times in *That Smell*, is borrowed from Hemingway's short story, "The Snows of Kilimanjaro." But what appears to have struck Ibrahim most about Hemingway is the American writer's commitment to the quotidian, to the truth of what he sees and hears. Ibrahim proves that this style, unbuttressed by commentary, could make its own revolutionary statement. (Equally interesting, of course, is what Ibrahim doesn't take from Hemingway: macho posturing is not in his narrator's repertoire.)

The third central concern of these notebooks is with the varieties of realism. This was a live issue in Egyptian literary circles at the time. Socialist realism was a dominant mode of the previous decade, most notably in Abd al-Rahman al-

Sharaqwi's *The Earth* (1952), a novel of class conflict in a village of the Nile Delta. *The Earth* was celebrated by proponents of *engagé* literature and spawned a host of imitators. But by the early sixties, in the wake of Khrushchev's revelations, socialist realism was considered by many, even on the left, as the house style of Stalinism. Another strain of realism, what we might call classical realism, culminated in the novels of Naguib Mahfouz. His suite of historical fictions, *The Cairo Trilogy*, is a minute and comprehensive depiction of Egyptian life in the first half of the twentieth century, refracted through the prism of a well-to-do family. But the conventions of classical realism, which presume a relatively stable class system to anchor its ambitious survey of social life, were unable to represent the shifts brought about by Nasser's reforms. The explosion of a lower middle-class population, largely employed by the expansionist state, and the resultant consumer society with its characteristic entertainments (movies, television, popular clubs) and objects of desire (refrigerators, electronics, suits), proved too much new material to squeeze into the strictures of Mahfouzian technique. In order for realism to remain realistic—this is Ibrahim's insight—it would have to become experimental.

In this sense, *Notes from Prison* can be read as a late episode in the debate between Realism and Modernism among intellectuals such as Georg Lukács, Berthold Brecht, and Walter Benjamin during the 1930s and '40s—the great age of speculation about the relationship between politics and literature. Those debates were still alive in the pages of *La Nouvelle Critique*, albeit in simplified form, and both Lukács and Brecht make appearances in Ibrahim's reading diary. For these writers the chief question was how to create a modern art form that would, in Marx's words, force mankind "to face with sober senses the real conditions of their lives and their relations with fellow men"— with the ambition, ultimately, to transform those conditions. If this goal now seems grandiose, that speaks to the reduced place literature holds in our own life rather than a flaw in the ambition. Ibrahim's response to this question, as evidenced by the *Notes* and his novel, was to focus on the terrain of the everyday. His fiction suggests that it is within the workday routine of gossip, casual consumption, and bodily experience— washing, eating, sex—that politics are most immediately felt and known. This is true even or especially when what one feels most of all is the absence of politics. It is his concern for the quotidian that seems to explain Ibrahim's notes on the films of Italian Neo-Realism and cinema verité. And indeed the narrator of *That Smell* acts as a kind of camera, recording the life around him while abstaining from comment.

Except in a few cases, Ibrahim did not have access to the texts mentioned in the *Notes* in the original language, or even in translation. He did not read the novels or poems, and did not see the films that he worried over for hundreds of pages. Instead, he imagined them as they were described or excerpted in the pages of Cairo's cultural supplements, French journals, and American magazines. (For this edition, I have tried to locate the works cited by Ibrahim, but have based my translations on the Arabic of the *Notes*, even when that version is different from the original.) Ibrahim's Hemingway is, in this sense, a dream of Hemingway, a famous style filtered through a scrim of secondary and tertiary literature, as well as translations. Perhaps this way of reading is what made it easy for Ibrahim to pick and choose what he found useful for his own work. To cobble together bits of Solzhenitsyn with bits of *The Green Hills of Africa* and bits of other things and come up with a style unique in Arabic literature. This search for models—"influence" is too passive a word to describe what Ibrahim is doing; it is more like bricolage—was made under severe restrictions. His library was limited to whatever the jailers picked up in the kiosks, or friends on the outside thought would be good for him to read. It is not by chance that in later work such as *The Committee* or *Zaat*, the protagonists are literary scavengers, collectors of ephemera, people who cannot help picking up the newspaper but never entirely believe what they read there.

In October of 2003, Ibrahim was given the Arab Novel Award, an honor bestowed by the Egyptian Ministry of Culture. To the surprise of many in the audience, familiar with his reputation as a dissident, Ibrahim attended the ceremony and delivered a now legendary speech. Instead of a gracious acceptance, his speech was an uncompromising attack on the Mubarak regime. In Egypt, Ibrahim observed, "We no longer have any theater, cinema, scientific research, or education. Instead, we have festivals and the lies of television." He went on, "Corruption and robbery are everywhere, but whoever speaks out is interrogated, beaten, and tortured." In view of this "catastrophe" Ibrahim had no choice but to refuse the prize, "for it was awarded by a government that, in my opinion, lacks the credibility to bestow it." A little less than eight years later, that regime—or at least its chief officer—was toppled. The role of artists and intellectuals in the new Egypt is far from clear. The state's powers of coercion are formidable and it is possible the old ways of doing things will survive with minor adjustments (increased subsidies for "Islamic" art, for example). But whatever the outcome of the recent revolts, *That Smell* will remain as an example of self-critical artistry at work in a moment of historical crisis. I hope it may also find an audience in translation.

ROBYN CRESWELL

THAT SMELL

This race and this country and this life produced me.... I shall express myself as I am.

—James Joyce, *Portrait of the Artist as a Young Man*

What's your address? the officer said. I don't have an address, I said. He looked at me, surprised. Then where are you going? Where will you live? I don't know, I said. I don't have anyone. He said, I can't let you go like that. I used to live by myself, I said. We have to know where you're living so we can come at night, he said. One of the policemen will go with you. And so we went into the street, the policeman and I, and I looked around curiously. It was the moment I'd been dreaming of for years and I searched myself for some feeling that was out of the ordinary, some joy or delight or excitement, but found nothing. People walked and talked and acted as if I'd always been there with them and nothing had happened. The policeman said, Let's take a taxi, and I saw that he wanted to have an easy time while I paid. We went to my brother's place and he said to me on the stairs that he was traveling and had to lock up, so we went downstairs and then to my friend's house. My friend said, My sister's here, I can't let you in. We went back down to the street. The policeman was getting annoyed. His eyes had a mean look and I figured that he wanted a few piastres. We can't go on like this, he said, let's go to the

19

station. At the station there was another policeman. You're a problem, he said. We can't let you go. I sat across from him and set my bag on the floor and lit a cigarette and when it was night he said there was nothing he could do. He called in a third policeman and said, Put him in the holding pen. So they led me to a cell with a fourth policeman standing by the door. He patted me down and took my money and put it in his pocket and pushed me into a big room with a wooden bench all around the walls and I sat down on the bench. There were a lot of men there and the door kept opening to let more in. I felt something in my knee. I put my hand down and sensed something wet. I looked at my hand and found a big patch of blood on my fingers and in the next moment saw swarms of bugs on my clothing and I stood up and noticed for the first time big patches of blood smeared on the walls of the cell and one of the men laughed and said to me, Come here. Some of the men were sitting on the ground and one of them had spread a ratty blanket on the ground and I found a little space on the edge and sat there with my chin on my knees. The man with the blanket said to me, Why don't you sleep? But there was no room for me, so I said, I'd rather just sit like this. Another one asked me, Drugs? No, I said. Robbery? No, I said. Murder? No. Bribery? No. Counterfeiting? No. So the man got quiet and confused and began looking at me with a strange look. I started to shiver with cold so I got up to walk around, then sat back down. I got tired of sitting and shifted my position. One of the men took out a blanket he had folded beneath him and got ready to sleep. I amused myself chasing the bugs scurrying across the floor and killing them. Then I dropped my head abruptly to my chest. I didn't want them to see my face. They had begun to fall asleep. In front of me, an old man lay on the bench. The policeman opened the door and called over to him, saying, There's someone here for you. The old man came back carrying a blanket and a pillow and stretched out on the bench, covering himself with the blanket and resting his head on the pillow and soon he was asleep, breathing heavily, unbothered by the bugs. Next to him a man sat looking right at me with his hands shoved into the pockets of his open jacket, which showed his bare chest. He wasn't wearing anything underneath the jacket. This man let out a strange and horrible howl then stood up and came over, staring at me and laughing in my face and then sat down next to me. He stared into space, confused. He howled. A big young man got up and hit him in the face. The madman raised his arms to protect his face and said, Don't hit me. The young man hit him and hit him and I heard the sound of bones cracking. He fell down where he was and he was breathing hard and the others laughed. The man with the blanket gathered up the blanket and spread it over himself and a chubby kid sleeping next to him. Before the blanket covered him, I saw the kid's face. He had pink skin and pouty lips. He was deep in sleep with his knees drawn up. The man spread the lower part of the blanket on top of him, then wiggled close. I watched his arm beneath the blanket moving across the kid's body, taking off his pants. The man's leg pressed against the kid's back. The big young man who had beaten up the madman sat close by. He followed what was going on beneath the blanket and every so often he raised his eyes to meet with mine. Soon the movements under the blanket stopped and the kid got up, throwing off the cover and rubbing sleep out of his eyes while looking down between his legs. I dozed off. I woke up, still sitting. I didn't see the big young man, then noticed his leg beneath the blanket. He was asleep with the kid in his arms. I stood up and walked around and the blanket twitched and the young man gathered it up, wrapping it around himself, and the kid lay there with nothing to cover his legs and the darkness began to lighten. I watched the early morning light come in and at last they opened the cell so we could wash up. They made the kid clean the yard. The others brought food and had breakfast and the kid came to the door and said, Didn't you leave anything for me? And the young man said, No. The policeman began to read off names and I heard my name and got my bag and went out and found my sister waiting for me with yesterday's policeman. He gave me a little notebook with my name and picture in it and my sister and I went out into the street. Do you want something to drink? she said. I want to walk, I said. She took me to an apartment in Heliopolis and I took some clean clothes and went into the bathroom and shut the door behind me and took off my clothes and stood naked beneath the showerhead. Then I rubbed my body with soap and turned the shower on. I lifted my head and fixed my eyes into the little eyes of the showerhead. The water pouring from it made me blink. I looked down and watched the soap and the water running off my body and onto the floor and into the drain. I rubbed my body with soap again and again I watched the water mixing with the soap and carrying it into the drain. I closed my eyes and stood still beneath the water. Then I turned off the tap and used a towel to dry my body slowly and dressed and walked out and lit a cigarette. My sister said, Let's go to the cinema, so we did. It was a movie about birds that kept getting bigger and multiplying until they became very wild and went after people and attacked children. I got a terrible headache. We went back to the apartment and my sister busied herself with cleaning. She went from the living room to the kitchen to the bedroom while I smoked and kept away from the window. I took off my clothes and stretched out on the bed. The bell rang so I got up and opened the door and it was the policeman who was knocking. Just a moment, I said. I went quickly to my room and brought the notebook and he wrote his name by the date and left. I went back to the bed and threw myself on top of it and lit a cigarette and stared at the ceiling. The policeman came back. I stayed stretched out on the bed without sleeping. I smoked a lot. In the morning I got up and dressed and went out. I bought a sandwich and all the morning's papers and caught a metro and watched the car doors closing. I was in the car next to the women's car and I started examining the women one by one. Their hair was combed in a very compli- cated way and their faces were heavy with paint. I got off at Emergency Station and there was a man lying on the sidewalk next to the wall. He was covered with bloody newspapers and a group of women had gathered in the street, wearing black sheets and waving their hands and ululating over him in grief. I got on a bus going to Mona's house. Her mother met me and I kissed her hand. She didn't recognize me at first, then we sat down to talk and I had to tell her about her husband. I said that I had been with him until the end.

I was sitting next to him, my hand cuffed to his. We were in the back of the van with the rest of the vans behind us. He knew what would happen but said nothing. He hummed snatches of an old love song over and over. The wind was stinging and there was nothing to protect us from the cold. I began shivering and my teeth chattered. We couldn't see the road. We talked about Hemingway. In the darkness, I saw him take a comb from his pocket and run it through his hair, which was going white. I knew he dyed his hair to hide the white. Silence fell over the car. In front of us, Ahmed had wrapped his head with a towel. He was moaning. Whenever his guts shivered, his head ached. It was dawn when we arrived and they forced us out with sticks and we sat on the ground, shaking with cold and fear. He was the tallest one. I heard a voice say, There he is, and they beat him on the head and said, Put your head down, you dog. They began calling people in, then they called him in, and that was the last time I saw him.

She said, You know, I got a letter from him before that where he said the whole thing would blow over soon. I said to her that he'd told me he'd never been able to sleep with Mona in his arms and that he used to smack his hands together and say, I'll get out before the rest of you. He wanted to get out at any price. Mona's mother looked around helplessly and closed her swollen eyelids over her eyes. She dropped her head onto her short, fleshy body. She signaled for me to come close and whispered, Did he really love me? And I said to her, Of course.

What could I say, what was the point of going into it after it was over, and who knows what goes on inside another person anyway? They say some people are made for love and some aren't. Others say love doesn't exist except in novels. As for him, he told me once about a woman whose family chased him away with clubs because he was from a differ-

ent religion. There was another woman, but she died unexpectedly. He discovered that a third had agreed with her husband to have a child no matter what. The husband was more than forty-five, approaching fifty, and he wanted a child. One day we were out in the sun together and he was distracted by his thoughts. I chatted away while he sank into his thoughts, ignoring me. Maybe he was working it out in his mind.... But once I was walking next to him down some stairs and we reached the ground floor when we heard a sharp, quick, continuous sound on the stairs. Then a tall young woman appeared, standing in front of the elevator. Sunlight fell from the staircase windows onto her face. She looked at us and she was laughing for some reason and her hair was wild and her cheeks were red. She wouldn't stand still. He stepped down next to me and his eyes were on her and I heard him give a hot sigh.

She got up and went to her room and came back carrying a little wallet from which she removed a few sheets of paper and handed me a worn sheet of paper and said, He wrote this poem for me before we were married.

She was always lost in thought and when he asked what she was thinking she said: About life and death. And he wrote:

> I am sad, child
> sad and alone
> I lie in my bed
> my cold dead bed
> with no one to speak with
> with all the books read
> with no one to laugh with
> with no tears to shed
> this is death

but more terrible
for the dead have no thoughts
unless the worm has thoughts
but the lonely man thinks
and desires and gazes and chases
without knowing what he chases
it is life and death
it is not life at all
though I haven't died yet
quiet! here are steps
human steps
coming closer and closer
are they real? yes! no! maybe!
yes! they ring the bells
I hear the human steps
I hear the human voices
alight with laughter
a friend? more than one
many friends, child
I am not sad anymore, child
but afraid
they will go and leave me again
to life and death!

And the bell rang and Sakhr came in and he had shaved his mustache and combed his hair and carried all the morning papers under his arm. The bell rang again and a well-dressed young man came in. Mona's mother said, pointing toward Sakhr, This is a friend of my husband. And the young man said, I know him. Sakhr leaped up and put on his glasses and began pacing the room. There were some English and French books on the shelves and he began leafing through them, then placed a hand on his hip and carried one of these books over to the window and began leafing through its pages while observing the well-dressed young man from time to time over his glasses.

It must have been one of his happiest moments to discover there was someone who knew him for some reason. In the past he thought everyone knew him, then gradually he discovered the truth. The first time I saw him he was bare-chested, walking with slow steps and occasionally raising a finger to fiddle with his mustache. In those days, world leaders sported a variety of mustaches and it was no accident that each was distinct from the others. These mustaches turned out to be a trick. The men who wore them were gone and so was their fashion. They left nothing in the heart. They never had. And he began to beat his head against the steel door until it nearly split, crying.

Through the window I saw a girl in the house opposite embrace another girl, kissing her on the lips. Then a girl who was blind in one eye came into the room and cried and while she cried, Sakhr stroked her hair with his hand. And Mona's mother said that the girl was like that, that as soon as she saw a man, she cried. Finally, Mona came home from school. I said to her, I'm a friend of your father and she gave me a suspicious look. I took her to the club. There were other children there and I asked them to take her into the water with them, since I didn't know how to swim, and they took her away. She ran and played and was happy. There was a piece of wood that helped with swimming and she grabbed onto it. But another little girl, a fat girl, took the piece of wood from her and floated on top of it. Mona held on to the piece of wood. The little fat girl grabbed her hair and pushed her away from the piece of wood, taking the piece of wood and swimming on top of it. Mona was a long way from the edge of the pool. I ran quickly toward her. She was bobbing up and down in the water and gasping for air and her eyes were wide with fear and I called out to her but she sank beneath the water and didn't reappear. One of the swimmers swam to help her and dragged her up, carrying her to me, and I took her home. While we were climbing the stairs, she said, If someone is there, I'm going to say you're my father. Don't say you aren't. We went into the house. Her mother was getting dressed, so I waited. Then my eyes fell on the wall clock. I jumped up and rushed for the door and rushed into the street. The policeman would arrive at any moment. I reached my room, gasping for air, and found a letter waiting for me. I checked to see who had sent it. It was from Nagwa. I read the letter slowly, then I lit a cigarette and stretched out on the bed and read the letter again. She was wondering if we might meet again after all these years. I closed my eyes to see what I could remember of how she looked: her affectionate eyes, her tender mouth. The bell rang and I got up to open the door. It was the policeman. I asked him to wait and came back to the room with the notebook for him to sign. He left and I kept the notebook in my pocket for next time. The bell rang again. When I opened the door Nagwa was there. I embraced her. She hugged me back violently, pressing her whole body against my body. But I didn't press against her, I pushed her away to look at her. Then I led her into the room and turned off the light and sat on the bed and pulled her down next to me. Then I pulled her toward me and kissed her on her lips. She pulled her face away and said, Talk to me. I didn't want to talk. I stroked her face. It was hot and soft. She pulled her face away, saying, Talk, say what happened. I put my hand over her mouth and pulled her head toward me and kissed her, gripping her lips between my lips. She bit me back in the same way, rough and unpracticed. Then she pulled away.

This is how it always was. The first time I kissed her, she acted shy. I was sitting next to her and the light was falling on her cheek and we had stopped talking. I rested my head on her shoulder and she didn't object. I kissed her on the cheek, then on the lips. When we'd gathered a little more courage, she gripped my lower lip and bit down on it hard. It hurt. I wanted to feel her soft lip in my mouth. I couldn't get enough of it. If I could have held her in my arms all day, I would have. I felt the heat in her face, in her thighs. Every time after that I would make her stand up naked and contemplate her thighs. They were beautiful and soft and dark. I would ask her to bare her forearms so I could kiss them and feel them against my body. But she hesitated. We would lie pressed together in the dark to forget the world, to forget everything. We thought of nothing, feared nothing, and when my cheek brushed her cheek, when our noses touched, when our heads rested against each other, when our eyes stared at the same place on the ceiling, then nothing else had any importance. Soon I would move my head and my lips would sneak over to her lips. We shared delicate kisses and rough kisses and then she would pull her head back and sigh. The first time she held me violently and said, Where were you all this time? Another time she said, Lover. I was quiet. The word echoed in my ear for the first time. I didn't trust myself. But soon she turned away and said, I want to sleep. I lay on my back, eyes up on the ceiling, hoping she would turn and embrace me but soon I felt her regular breathing, the contented and peaceful breathing of someone sleeping. So I turned and raised myself up to look at her. Her head rested on her arm while she slept. Her hair was spread across her neck and her other arm rested on her side. I let my look linger all over her body, then dropped back on the bed.

She stretched out next to me and laid her cheek on my hand, offering me her face lit by a little moonlight. She said, I'll do the talking. She talked for a long time, then stopped. I told her I was worn out, that I had always wanted her. I pulled her toward me but she pulled away. I asked her to bare her forearm and she did. I kissed her forearm and her shoulder in the moonlight but soon she said, It's cold, and she covered them. Then she stretched out on her back. She must have been thinking the same thing I was thinking. Something was missing, something was broken. She said, I want to sleep. I pulled her toward me and kissed her. My lips wandered from cheek to ear, kissing her there until she shivered and raised her eyes to mine and smiled and said, And this, where did you learn this?

How could she remember while I had forgotten? When my lips climbed up her thigh and I kissed her there for the first time and she looked at me with a mixture of pleasure and surprise and shyness, she said, Where did you learn this?

I reached my hand toward her chest but she pushed it away and said, No. I rolled away, then stretched out beside her. I waited for her to turn and embrace me but she didn't. I was awake. I felt the pain between my legs. I got up and went to the bathroom. I got rid of my desire, then came back and stretched out beside her. I slept and woke and slept again and when I opened my eyes it was morning and she had already put her clothes on. I'm leaving now, she said. When will I see you? I asked. I'll come by, she said. I stayed there stretched out on the bed, then finally got up and washed. I put some powdered soap in a basin of water and stirred it until the foam rose, then put my dirty clothes in. My sister and her fiancé came by. I put my clothes on and we went out and I bought the morning papers. In the entrance to the building we met a friend of my sister and her uncle and we went to a café. My sister's fiancé said, We want to be happy for you. That will take time, I said. Why? he asked. Love isn't easy, I said. He shrugged and said, Here's my advice, love comes after marriage. The uncle said, I've been married five times. I left them and went to see Sami at his place. I was brought into the living room and waited for him a long time. A little girl came in whom I recognized as his daughter. She walked up to me. I felt uncomfortable. I needed to use the toilet and I broke wind and the little girl smelled it. Caca smell, she said. I pretended not to smell it. But again she said, Caca smell. So I started sniffing all around, saying, Where? until the smell went away. Finally I gave up on Sami and got up and left. The traffic was terrible. I went to the offices of the magazine but no one was there. A radio was playing loudly in the street—it was a song in English about children and I realized that Muhammed Fawzi's new song was the same song. I got on the metro and the crowds were horrendous and I almost suffocated. I looked at the faces of tired women with eyeliner running down their faces. I went to Samia's house and found them eating. Samia smiled when she saw me and said she had waited for me for a long time before starting to eat. Really? I almost said. I asked about her boy and she said he was sleeping. I felt myself smiling. Her smile was simple and sincere. I hadn't thought that she was so simple and so graceful.

So what? She has her husband and her child and there's no place for anyone else in her life and soon I'll leave and that will be the end of everything.

Every now and then she sighed hotly and said, O Lord. I said to her, If Freud heard you, he would have something to say about that. Lots of things, she said. We finished eating and she stood up. She was wearing a light shirt with nothing under it and just beneath her armpit I saw the side of her breast where it bulged out from her chest. I was surprised it didn't droop. It was milky white. I looked away and into her eyes, so frank and so straightforward. She went in to sleep and I slept too and when I woke up I looked for her in her room. Her bed was on the far side of the room and she was lying on her back with her head turned away from me, gazing at the wall opposite, with her son at her chest, still sleepy and looking around in confusion. Her leg was bare—it was milky white—and she quickly covered it. She got up and put on an orange skirt and we sat on the balcony and she said that her little boy liked me. I loved her easy, honest voice, her simple gestures. I told her that I felt like an old man. I hardly smiled or laughed. All the people I saw on the street or on the metro were unhappy, unsmiling. What was there to be happy about? We talked about books. She said she'd stopped reading a while ago, when her boy was born. I asked if she had read *The Plague*. I felt as though a lot rode on her answer but she said, No. I was about to tell her that I envied her simplicity and her grace. I told myself that I would say so when we said goodbye. I looked at my watch. I had to go. I stood up and so did she and I said to her in a low voice, You know, you're really strange. She looked at me in surprise. Today, I finally figured you out, I said. She bent over her little boy and busied herself straightening his clothes and I couldn't see her eyes very well. Her husband came home and I said goodbye to both of them. They accompanied me to the stairs. At the garden gate, I turned around. She was going back into her nice cool home and I watched her orange skirt disappear behind the door. I walked back to the apartment and saw a nice-looking girl walking next to the train rails as if she was having trouble with her shoes. I went into the building. The light was on in the wood-paneled room by the entrance and the door was open. I peeked in and saw my sister's friend Husniyya. I went up to my room and my sister came. I said to her, Samia's nice. Then I said, Is she happy with her husband? Of course, she said. I bet she doesn't love him, I said. Impossible, she said. Where else will she find a man like that, as far as personality and position? And she said they had met before getting married.

So what if they had met before getting married.... She was twenty-seven, she'd waited for her prince a long time with no luck.... She had no privacy at home, she slept in a room that was like a living room. She could never close the door and be alone and take off her clothes, for example. She couldn't look at her body in a mirror. She couldn't stand the meaningful looks of her father and her mother every night. There was nothing to talk about except the husband that kept not coming. She was blamed for not being able to catch one herself. Then one night she met him at a girlfriend's house. The next day her friend told her that he wanted to marry her and after a ten-minute walk home, at the door to that house with its peeling paint, she said to her friend, Why not? Maybe he was the lover she was waiting for. Maybe all this talk about love and making eyes at each other and heaving sighs was only for books. Maybe she had found happiness with him. Maybe.... The word that hangs over every new marriage. Maybe he was the man she was waiting for. Maybe this was love. One year later the child came and now she was stuck forever. There was nothing to do but submit.... And that time when the radio was playing, when I noticed her eyes go thoughtful and her face become full of sadness.... What happened after the marriage? I imagined them next to each other on the bed, one of them bored and resentful, always feeling that something inside her was unmoved, that her flesh no longer quivered, that some deep well went unplumbed.

Do you know what love is? I said. She looked at me in surprise. My question was silly and naïve. Of course, she said. Do you love your fiancé? I said. I do, she said. When we got engaged I couldn't stand him, but later on I loved him. Her voice was raised. Why are you upset? I said. That's just how I talk, she said. Then she said she wanted to shower but that if she did her hair would be a mess and she'd have to go to the hairdresser again. The bell rang. I got my notebook and went to open the door but it was my sister's fiancé. Standing behind him was his friend, Husniyya. Husniyya said to my sister, Can you believe it, my fiancé is jealous of my uncle. He says I spend all my time with my uncle. My sister's fiancé said he had spent all day looking for a water heater and bought a refrigerator. Does anyone know someone traveling abroad who could bring me back a tape recorder? he said. Husniyya's uncle came and took them all to the cinema and I was left on my own at my desk. I tried to write. The bell rang and I rushed to the door hoping that something would happen, that someone would come. It was the clothes presser. The bell rang again. Opening the door, I was surprised to see Nihad and her father. They swept into the room and said, You must come to our house tomorrow. I said to Nihad, You've really changed. She smiled nicely and said, The last time you saw me, I was very young. They refused to sit down and said that Nihad's mother was waiting in the car and I said goodbye to them outside and then went back to my room. I smoked greedily, thinking, unable to write. She had looked at me very closely. I supposed she had heard a lot about me and must have been impressed. The bell rang a third time, a long and powerful ring. I got my notebook and went to the door and opened it and gave the notebook to the policeman, then went back to my room and turned the light off and lay down on the bed and went to sleep. I woke up startled by the sound of the bell. When I opened the door no one was there. I went back to my room and left its door open and went back to sleep. I got up early in the morning and shaved and dressed and took a clean shirt to the clothes presser and went back and changed, then went downstairs and looked for a place to have my shoes shined. I bought the papers and finally got on the metro. The conductor stopped to put a lump of opium in his mouth and sip some tea. Lucky man, I thought. He'd found a way to live that let him put on a brave face. He resumed driving very slowly. I wished he would speed up so that I wouldn't be late and the dust wouldn't ruin my elegant get-up. I got off a long way away from the house and caught a taxi and stopped it in front of the house. I looked up at the balconies and saw no one. So I climbed up to the top floor and found Nihad with her mother at the table. They hadn't seen the taxi. I sat down with them. Nihad was studying. I looked at her hard. Her lips were as I'd hoped. The lower one was curved and her teeth showed a little. Her voice was calm and graceful. Her mother asked what I was doing now. Her voice was rather loud. I told her I was writing. Are you writing stories? she said. Yes, I said. Out of books? No, I said, from my head. And Nihad said, You must be a big shot. I lit a cigarette. You should settle down, her mother said. America is wonderful, Nihad said. What do you think? I like some things and not others, I said. Forget all this and look out for yourself, she said. Then she said, Help me study. Her voice was very soft. I had had enough of loud voices. Can you believe what they did to my father? she said. They threw him out of his company after they took it away from him. She said they had conspired against him and accused him of fraud. Let's eat, they said, and we went down to the ground floor. We sat at the table and I took some salad and rice on my plate and Nihad asked me, Thigh or breast? My sister had warned me. Don't take a thigh, she said, you won't know how to eat it with a knife and fork. I don't know what got into me but I said to her, Give me the thigh. She put it in front of me and I grabbed the knife and fork and when I stuck the fork in the thigh flew up from my plate and landed in the salad bowl. That's not how chicken is eaten, Nihad said calmly. Eat it with your fingers. I said that my sister had warned me but I didn't pay attention to her warning. Her father ate his thigh with a knife and fork. The mother said that in Europe they

didn't eat the thigh with a knife and fork and after that I didn't
know how to eat. I made a mess of the macaroni and water-
melon. What do you think of the situation? they said. The father said that he'd met people coming from Russia and that
the poverty there was terrible. He said capitalism was better.
Who can argue with that? Nihad said forcefully. Then she said,
Do you believe in our Lord? I got up and washed my hands and
dried them on a towel and we went upstairs. They offered
cigarettes but I didn't feel like smoking. The father spoke on
the telephone. He wanted to buy the land next door. The
mother put her hand to her cheek and faded out. The father
came in to sleep and Nihad said, Are you tired? No, I said, and
we went back to studying. The father woke up and unrolled
the prayer mat in front of us and made his prayers, then sat
down next to us and they brought tea. How's Nihad doing? he
said. Very well, I said. Behind us they turned the television on
to a very high volume. The maid and the cook and the nanny
came in and sat on the floor to watch. Nihad was ignoring me
and watching the film. She said, Ahmad Ramzi is amazing. I
started to get tired. She got up and sat beside me. Her bare
forearm was next to me. She was careful not to touch. The
mother heard me explain a word in English and said, No, that's
not what it means. Then the father broke in, though he only
knew French. He said the word in French had a different meaning. I said nothing while the mother and father fought. The
mother asked me to support her version. Usually that's the
meaning, I said. No, the father said, giving me a look. More or
less, I said. Then the noise from the television got very loud.
Nihad said that a director had seen her that morning and said

that she looked like Lubna Abdel Aziz. Some visitors arrived and Nihad got up to welcome them and sat with them at the other end of the room. She talked with them very animatedly, then ignored them to watch Ahmad Ramzi. I had a splitting headache and got up to leave. One of the visitors looked at me inquiringly. I'm the son of so-and-so, I said. She laughed and pointed to her nose, then twirled an imaginary mustache, lifting its tips. The one with the big mustache? she said. Yes, I said. The mother shouted, Come here. I wondered if she was feeling bad for me and would give me five guineas. She signaled for me to follow her to her room. Her maid was sitting on a chair, a plump dark girl. My class of woman, I said to myself. I thought that if I spoke with the mother I could marry her. Then they could say they had helped me find a good wife, just the right kind for me. The mother handed me some rolled-up papers and said it was a bolt of fabric. I didn't know what to say. I had decided to say no if she offered me money, but I hadn't counted on an offer of fabric. I got annoyed and said no, but she insisted. You're like my son, she said. I didn't know what to do. I took it and told myself that anyway I had gotten a suit out of it. I went back to the living room and Nihad went with me to the stairs and I left the house, not looking up. I walked and my shoes filled with dust and I didn't care. I got on the metro. It was terrifyingly crowded. My clothes were crumpled. I didn't protest. At one stop the train was assaulted by tens of workers on their way home. They forced their way through the crowd and one of them stood in front of me. His eyes were bloodshot. Another leaned against a row of seats and stared from the window and began to fall asleep. When I looked at him again his head was bouncing along with the movement of the train and knocking into the seats while he fell deeper and deeper into sleep. When I got off I saw the same girl I had seen before, walking slowly next to the train rails. I went up to my room and put the key in the lock. It was the same door and the same key for all families of our class. I went in and took my clothes off and put my trousers on a hanger and hung them from the wall. Then I showered. Then I sat down at my desk and turned on the transistor. The roll of fabric was in front of me. I opened it. It was pajama fabric, not suit fabric. I lit a cigarette. My sister appeared and said, How much is left of the fifty piastres? I counted up my transportation costs, but didn't dare tell her about the ten piastres the taxi had cost. Her fiancé appeared and said he had stood for two hours outside the cooperative to buy meat. He said the situation was unbearable. You guys want to spread poverty, he said. There's no way for me to make money. If I build something, the government would take it away. Adel and his wife came and I offered him a cigarette and he said, I don't smoke and I don't drink coffee. He said that he only had a cup of tea in the morning, but that his bill at the office was thirty piastres a day because of the demands of his co-workers. Unlike them, he didn't take bribes. Too bad, his wife said. No one can talk to workers anymore, she said. Adel said that the chauffer of his uncle, Fahmy Bey, didn't get up until ten in the morning, although Fahmy Bey was up at dawn. He said to my sister's fiancé, I'll show you the best place to buy a soap dish. My sister said she needed a maid, but where could she find one? Her fiancé said that he had ordered a Ronson lighter, which was on its way from Beirut. We have to go now, they all said. They went and I was left at my desk, smoking. Then I got up and turned the light off and stood by the window, breathing in the air. My window looked out on the backs of several apartments. I could see only a little stretch of the street. I stuck my head out and twisted my neck so I could see the lit-up shops and the people coming and going. Then I tired of this and pulled my head back in and rested my arm on the window ledge. Across from me there was a darkened window. It lit up suddenly, showing a young woman slowly removing her clothes. Eventually she was completely naked. She threw herself on a bed in the corner of the room and lay face down, her back turned to the light. I stared at her shapely body and the dark shadows the light left along her curves. Then the bell rang. I got my notebook and stalled for a moment, lighting a cigarette and picking up the pack to take with me. The bell rang again and I went quickly to the door. I opened it and gave the policeman the notebook while taking out the pack of cigarettes. I gave him a cigarette, then he left and I went back to my room and tossed the notebook on the desk. I glanced over at the window opposite. It had gone dark. I stretched out on the bed and smoked the cigarette all the way down, then flicked it out the window and slept. In the morning I bought a magazine and a small glass of milk and some bread. I went home and boiled the milk and put some sugar in it, then dunked the bread in the milk while reading the magazine. Then I went out and caught the metro. It stopped just before Emergency Station and all the passengers got off. Several cars were turned over on their sides next to the rails. Their blackened innards stuck out. I walked to the café where Magdi liked to sit. He was there by himself in a corner. He said, We must affirm our existence. I examined the wrinkles that had dug themselves all over his face. He said, They're all sons of bitches. Then he said, With the people, you're strong, on your own, you're weak. His face crumpled.

Looking at him you wouldn't know if he was full of hate or pain. Is there anyone who doesn't hate, doesn't suffer? From a desire for power and from cowardice? From the loss of love and the failure to love? From contempt for others and a need for company? From being brutalized and behaving brutally? From suffering pain and the joy of causing it? From complete self-confidence and the conviction one is a failure? From love-lessness and the exploitation of love (which you use like bricks to build your own house)? From the belief that everyone admires you and has faith in you and from abandonment? At the beginning it was a noble cause. Now it's a curse. No more sympathy for others.... When he stood there with his back dripping blood he was resolute, unbreakable. He took pleasure in standing firm. But no one cares about all that anymore. The world has changed. It's no accident the words on his lips don't mean what they used to. Some of them are practically meaningless.... He was in on the game, he understood its rules, he played by them. But they turned the rules against him and now he's the one weeping. The worst thing is to begin searching for yourself when it's too late.... He said that he'd never fallen in love and that he always believed he was better than the rest— maybe he was, there's nothing to prove otherwise, and he gave all he had—but he lost. It was a game without mercy and in fact without rules, where you couldn't distinguish right from wrong, where the winner wasn't always the one in the right, but the cleverest, the trickiest, the luckiest.

I left him and went to the offices of the magazine. I walked down a long hallway, looking in all the rooms, but no one was there. As I approached the last room at the end of the hallway I saw a woman seated at a desk with her cheek in her hand. There were tears in her eyes. I turned around and went back the way I had come. I walked toward the metro and got on, taking a seat next to the window, and as we pulled away from Midan Ramses another train pulled alongside us heading in the same direction. It was full of soldiers returning from Yemen. They were shouting from the windows and calling out and waving their hands. When our train pulled up across from them and they saw the passengers they grew more excited. The passengers looked at them coldly, without interest, and slowly the soldiers became less and less excited. Our train had pulled ahead of theirs by now and I turned around to look. The soldiers' hands hung from the windows of the train and I saw one throw his cap on the ground. I got off at my house and saw the pretty girl who walked next to the train rails every day. Now I saw that she was a cripple. I bought some food and went upstairs and found the door of the apartment open and my neighbor inside, fixing the lock to his room. I went in and ate, then smoked and slept. I woke up to find that my sister had come in. I went into the bathroom and undressed and released the water onto my body. I heard the sound of a doorknob falling onto the floor tiles. I turned off the water, dried myself, dressed, then came out of the bathroom. There was a constant knocking sound. I talked to my sister and combed my hair. I heard the knocking again. I realized that the sound was coming from the other side of the wall. I said to my sister that we always did that when we wanted to speak to each other, or to warn each other.

It happened every morning. We opened our eyes to the sound of regular knocks coming from the other side of the wall. We jumped out of bed, still half asleep, and tidied up, trying to remember not to forget anything. Then we squatted on our heels next to the wall, shivering with cold. The knocking would stop and we would wait. Then we heard the sound of their steps on the floor tiles, the jangling of chains and keys. When the key slammed into the lock, we flinched. Then they came in. Our eyes flew to their eyes, hard beyond description. Quick, sharp, frightening sounds attacked our ears. Their hands—fat and coarse and cruel—squeezed our hearts. The walls made four corners. The door was shut. The ceiling was near. No help.

I went out to the living room and glanced toward my neighbor's apartment. The glass door was shut and I made out his shadow behind the glass. He was pounding it with his hand. I saw the key on the ground and picked it up and put it in the door and opened it. He told me through his tears that he'd forgotten to take the key when he went in and had been knocking for an hour. My sister said she had to visit Husniyya and see her fiancé. We left. Husniyya's mother welcomed me, saying: You have to get settled. And to my sister she said, Make him get married and he'll calm down. Husniyya's fiancé came in and said that he had arranged his desk at the ministry in the most wonderful way. A thick pane of glass covered the top, a foreign notepad was on the right, an ivory inkwell—the kind you can't get anymore—was in the middle, on the left were his urgent files, and over his head was a plaque with a Quranic verse. I said the sun was almost down and I had to go. I rushed home but the policeman was already on the stairs. You're late, he said. I pulled out a pack of cigarettes but he shook his head.

43

You could spend tonight in prison, he said. So I took out ten piastres and he walked with me up to the apartment. I brought him the notebook and he signed it and left. I slowly took off my clothes, washed my face, then prepared a cup of coffee and tidied up my desk, wiping away the dust that had gathered on it. I grabbed the pen. But I couldn't write. I picked up a magazine and there was an article in it about literature and how it should be written. The writer said that Maupassant said that the artist must create a world that is more beautiful and more simple than our world. He said that literature must be optimistic and alive with the most beautiful sentiments. I stood and went to the window, looking over at yesterday's window. It was closed. I went back to the desk and picked up the pen but couldn't write. I shut my eyes and imagined the girl from yesterday, her plump white body on the bed in front of me, freshly washed hair, me kissing every part of her. I rubbed my cheek along her leg and rested it on her breast. I put my hand between my legs. I began playing with myself and at last I sighed. Then I threw myself back in the chair, exhausted, staring at the page with a blank look. A little while later I got up and stepped carefully over the traces I'd left on the floor under the chair and went into the bathroom to wash my socks and shirt and hang them by the window. Then I turned off the light, leaving the door open so I could hear the policeman when he came. I lit a cigarette and stretched out on the bed and slept. In the morning I went to my brother's house. Wrinkles marched over his face and his skin was splotched with white. Everything's ruined since the workers joined the Administrative Committees, he said, and suggested we go upstairs to see his older daughter.

My brother built the villa fifteen years ago and he said it was his wife who bought the land, which was when he realized she had money. My father was alive at the time. He would come every day to supervise the construction. We lived in a little room. My brother finished the construction and rented out the first floor and lived on the second, then married off his older daughter and rented the third floor to her. When his younger daughter married he emptied the first floor and rented it to her and stayed on the middle floor with his wife. In the beginning, he spent an hour each day pruning the hedges in his garden and smoking his pipe.

She asked if I would read to her husband. Her husband said that Sheikh Abdel Basit said that one prayer at al-Aqsa Mosque was worth a thousand piety points. They suggested we go downstairs to see the younger daughter. She met us at the door with her child in her arms. His eyes were close together. Isn't my son beautiful? she said. She laughed, then laughed a little more to prompt her husband. He was standing next to her, fingering the stars of his uniform. He said that if a private so much as opened his mouth, he'd crack him across the face and shut him up. Then he said, It's time for you to get married. Do as I did, he said. The most important thing about a girl is where she comes from. They turned on the television. My brother straightened his robe and smiled and said, Just watch this film. It was a story about a young woman who left a man her age and fell in love with an older man. When the film was over, my brother gave us a superior look. He took me to his room and shut the door and took out some old folders, then sat at his desk and lit a pipe. He showed me some stories he'd written and others he'd translated, a bunch of articles entitled "Dear Sir," a book on body building, another on the battles of the Second World War, a third about Prince Omar Toussoun, an old photograph of himself with a little hat and pipe in his garden, and another picture of him with a German girl. He said it was from the days of Rommel's advance on Alexandria, when he'd started to learn German. Then he showed me a third picture of him at the offices of an American company and another of him at the offices of an Egyptian importer. I wish I had a little young thing, he said. And he said he had never been in love. And he said that yesterday he had wanted to sleep with his wife but she wouldn't let him because he had made her buy fruit with her own money, but when he gave her two guineas she opened up. He gathered the papers and photographs and put them back in their folders. I'm finished now, he said. I'm going to raise rabbits. They called us to eat. Afterward, I left and went to the magazine and met Sirri. He said he'd like to help me but that under the circumstances there was nothing he could do. Have you read my pieces? he said. I'm the only one who writes like that now. Fuad is a trifler, he said, and would you believe he claimed I was his disciple? I left him and went to Sami's office at the end of the corridor. This time he was there. I have no idea what you've been writing lately, he said. I stood next to his desk while he wrote something. He look up at me, puzzled. I won't keep you, he said. Come see me in a couple days. I went out to the street and walked to the metro. I saw an extremely pretty girl through the window of an airlines office. I rode the metro home. There were no empty seats, so I stood and looked at the people. In the women's car I saw a woman in profile. She was staring from the window wearing a sleeveless white dress.

She looked exceptionally clean. She must have taken a shower before heading out. Her hair was long and silky and there was no way she'd had it done at a hairdresser. I noticed a little girl next to her. When she turned her whole face toward me and I saw her wine-dark complexion, my chest clenched. Her face had no shadow, no paint. I found myself staring into her eyes, which were large and clear, and for a moment I lost myself.

Her eyes were stars in silent space where I was swimming and sinking. It was night. Our eyes met and hers glimmered in the light and I saw myself in their wide-open whites and I saw her in their black depths. Her bare arm was next to me. Its skin was dark with a little red mixed in. It seemed warm. I wanted to touch it at the plump joint just below the shoulder. Her white blouse was airy and she wasn't wearing an undershirt. I could see the points of her nipples beneath the blouse where they brushed against the silk. The skin of her face was soft, her lips were full and parted, the lower one making a little arch, and they were dark-colored as though scorched by some fire. When she looked at me she smiled and let her look linger. I got dizzy. When I pulled her toward me she went still, then pushed me away. We were sitting in the dark. She reached out her hand and played with my hair. It crept to the collar of my shirt, then to my back. She caressed my back with her palm. I drew her toward me and buried my face in her neck, taking pleasure in the softness of her skin on my cheek. I breathed in her clean smell and raised my head and kissed her lips and was lost. When I returned to the attack, she pushed me away. I studied her moods. When she tightened her lips and would not speak, I went mad wanting to know why. When she looked vulnerable or pitiable, I adored her. When I sat in front of her, looking at her face, her hands, her legs, I almost wept with desire. It hurt to look at her bright eyes, her mouthwatering cheeks. It hurt when

my fingers crept over her arm and my leg inched toward her leg and she
refused me. I was finally on the point of madness. I had almost given up
when she took me in her arms and let me touch her breasts and hands
and kiss her cheek and lips. But she was cold.

She turned her eyes away and didn't look at me again. I got
off at my stop and bought some food and went upstairs. The
light was on in the wood-paneled room used by Husaniyya's
uncle and the door was open. When I looked in I saw him
with his head in his hands, looking at a picture of a girl in a
gold frame on the small table in front of him. It was a picture
of Husaniyya. In the picture, her eyes were big and beautiful.
I moved away before he sensed I was there. I went up to my
room and took my clothes off and turned on the transistor,
but there were no songs or music and it started to crackle. I sat
and tried to write. The traces of my pleasure looked like black
spots on the floor. Hasan came in and I told him we needed
to get a woman right away. He said he would do his best, and
left. He came back in half an hour and said, My brother's on
the stairs with a girl. Make yourself scarce for a while. We told
her there were only two of us. I went to the kitchen and made
some tea. Hasan came in and said his brother and the girl were
in my room now. I carried the tea into the living room and put
it on the table, then sat at the table. Hasan lit a cigarette and
drummed his fingers on the table. Soon the door to the room
opened and Hasan's brother came out and I shook his hand.
I had never met him before. He was a big man in his forties.
Hasan went into the room and I offered his brother some tea.
He said, How are things? Very good, I said. I pointed to the
room and said, How is she? He shrugged. Not bad, he said. We

48

drove all over but it was so late she was the only one we found. Hasan came out and said to me, Your turn. I took him aside and said, I can't. He looked at me, surprised. What do you mean? I don't know, I said. I don't feel like it. He shook me. You've got to go in there, he said. This is a big deal. I said that I knew it was but that I couldn't. Come on, he said, and shoved me toward the door. I went in and locked the door behind me. Hasan's brother said from behind the door that the rubber was on the desk. I lit a cigarette and offered her one. She was sitting on the bed in her underclothes, wearing a cheap pink shirt with holes in it, like a white rag that had been dipped in blood and washed over and over but still kept the faded color of the blood. Her legs were bare. Her skirt was carefully folded on the desk. She said, I don't want to smoke, let's get on with it. Let's have a cigarette first, I said. What's your name? I want to get this over with, she said, and put her hand out to unbutton my pants. I turned her hand away gently and said, Just sleep with me tonight, then leave in the morning. Yeah, right, she laughed, and then pulled me toward her, trying to kiss me. I turned my mouth away from her face and stood up and took off my pants and underwear and picked up the rubber and began putting it on, but it ripped. I looked for another on the desk. There wasn't one. The girl said, I'm clean. I opened the door and called to Hasan, I need one, and he gave me one from his pocket and I put it on and I threw myself on top of her. She tried to kiss me so I moved my face away and finally got up and put my clothes on. The other two took her out and I sat down and lit a cigarette. Ramsi came and I told him I hadn't been able to sleep with the girl and he made fun of me. He had managed it. He met a girl in the street

49

and went home with her and turned off the lights. It took ten minutes, then he gave her twenty-five piastres and looked at his face in the mirror. It was red. Nothing is worth anything, he said. Then he left. Soon the policeman came and then I turned off the light and slept. In the morning I went out and had breakfast in the street. I didn't buy the papers. I went back to my room and my sister said my uncle was returning from Alexandria and that he was very sick and that I needed to go meet him. I went out and caught a metro, taking it to the station. I got off and crossed the square, passing through the entrance in the wall that surrounded the station. I found him standing on the platform. He looked just fine and his wife was standing next to him with an umbrella in her hand. His kids rushed to hail a taxi and they all got in and told me to meet them at home, so I got on the metro and went to meet them at their house and found him sitting on the sofa in his pajamas. His body seemed small and suddenly shrunken. I looked at his shoulders, which were thin beneath his t-shirt, and his little eyes, which were almost lost behind his thick glasses. His pajama pants were stained with big yellow blotches above the pouch between his legs. He said it had come on all of a sudden with shaking and a fever. They called the doctor, who said there was absolutely nothing wrong. He said his temperature had gone up in the night and that he thought he was going to die and sent for the doctor right away. The doctor said, Eat boiled vegetables and get a urine test. My uncle said he followed the doctor's orders for one day. The day after he said, I'm eating chicken. We got up to eat and he fell on the meat, devouring it with gusto. Give me some liver, he said. I left them and went out, catching a metro to my cousin's house. I told myself I would know the house by its blue windows, but when I got there I discovered they weren't blue as I'd imagined. They were just ordinary, uncolored glass. It was the sky that had sometimes made them seem blue. All the panes were cracked. The facade of the house was yellow and dirty. The gate to the garden was open, propped against the wall. The garden itself was untended and its paving stones were torn up here and there. I took the path leading to the front door. There was dog shit along the wall. I climbed the stairs with their crumbling steps and knocked at the door. My aunt's daughter opened it. At first I didn't recognize her. Her hair was unkempt and scraggly, with many strands of gray. Her eyes were dull and the skin of her face was brown. From the living room, I looked into the south-facing room. I went in and said, Where's the sewing machine you used to have here? She said, Do you still remember?

Of course I did. It was wintertime, after lunch. My father sat in the north-facing room with my aunt, looking out at the palace through the veranda's window. I went to him, wanting to sit on his lap, but he turned me away. He said I wasn't a little boy anymore. I turned back to the living room and walked through it to my cousin's room. She sat at the sewing machine and I watched as she worked the machine with her foot. Look at this, she said, the string broke at the first stitch. There's a devil in this machine. She bent over the machine after a glance in my direction. I turned toward the window, ears burning. I could see her white face with red cheeks even as I looked toward the closed window. It was only the glass that was closed. Beyond it was the sky. Brilliant rays of sun shone through the glass and lit up the mouth of the well in the garden below. Soon the servant boys would come and I'd go down with them to pump the water. We would steal a few flowers and shake the mango tree to no purpose, then run through the bedrooms and the cellar. This time I would hide from them in a room that was tucked away and only used during Ramadan, when the sheikhs recited there at night. When we left that evening my aunt would say goodbye at the door and turn on the light for the stairs. We would walk down the broad white steps and over the colored paving stones, open the garden's squeaky gate and go out into the wide and noiseless street. I would pick jasmine from the walls of the gardens.... My cousin's friend said something. She was standing just in front of the wardrobe's mirror, putting on lipstick. I wasn't looking at her. She was tall with green eyes. She'd only said one thing to me. When she came into the room she said, Hey. Then she turned to my cousin. But my cousin was talking to me when she said, Look at this. The little wardrobe was behind me. Each of its wooden panels was fixed with a bright mirror. A small brass chime hung from the middle keyhole, so that whenever the wardrobe was opened it made a pretty ringing sound. Inside the wardrobe were closed drawers with my cousin's things arranged in rows. I was happy because the wardrobe was closed. Without taking my eyes from the window, I could watch my cousin's fingers lightly touching the machine's handle, making the wheel spin noisily. She bent down, following the fabric as it moved beneath the needle. Her two braids fell over her chest. Her friend said to her, Will you ever finish? We're late. My cousin lifted her head and our gazes met and then she looked at her friend and said, This is the last part. I blinked and heard the ring of the small brass chime.

My sister came in and said, The city sewers are overflowing. Then an old relative of my cousin came in, panting. He could hardly see from behind his thick glasses. My cousin's face darkened. The old man said, Give me a shilling after I have some coffee. He took off his tarboosh and placed it beside him on the sofa and drank his coffee and then just sat there. My cousin went into her room and came back and asked if I had any change on me. I didn't have any change. They sent the cook to get two shillings for ten piastres. We sat and waited for him to come back without speaking. Then my cousin gave the old man his shilling and he got up and put his hat back on and said goodbye and left. My cousin said, He's a crafty old man. He only wheezes like that when he comes to see us. My sister said that he lived with his married son and that the son's wife encouraged her children to rip his clothes and hide his shoes and make a mess in his room. My cousin said, He'll drink up the shilling. My sister said, When he visits his daughter she leaves him in the living room and shuts her bedroom door on him. My cousin said, He'll spend the day drinking and begging from all his relatives.

Many years ago in that same room, my aunt sat in her white veil on the sofa, smoking, and next to her my father was still panting from the stairs and the heat. He used a handkerchief to wipe his bald head, fringed with white hairs. The cook came in and my aunt took out her purse and gave him a guinea and the cook left. My father said something and she shook her head. My father got up and walked toward the north-facing room out onto the veranda and lit his black cigarette and leaned his elbows on the veranda's ledge and smoked.

My sister said that Nihad was engaged to a director in the public sector. She told my cousin about the relative of Nihad who'd asked me if I was the son of the man with the pointed mustache and we laughed and my sister said Nihad's grandmother was sick and that her family couldn't stand her. Before my mother died she went months without leaving her bed and she would pee in it, my cousin said. And my sister said that the wife of another cousin had had a miscarriage in her sixth month. Lucky her, I said. My sister got mad at me and told me I had no feelings. She said I was the only one who wouldn't be able to come to her wedding because it would be after sunset. And she said that her friend Husniyya would get married a week after her and then Husniyya's uncle would go back home. And she said that Husniyya's uncle had lived with Husniyya since he left his wife. And she said that his wife never took off her mourning clothes, that according to him even her underclothes were black. My cousin's dog approached me, wagging his head. I put my hand down to pet him and he immediately went to sleep on his back and peed all over the floor. They said that was how he was these days, as soon as he slept on his back, he peed. I went home and undressed and prepared a cup of tea and sat down and read a book about Van Gogh. I must have dozed off, because I imagined that I met my father. He seemed tired. He sat cross-legged on his bed, frowning. I didn't know what to say to him. It had been a long time since I tried to see him. He had been there the whole time, but I didn't think to visit. I woke up suddenly at the sound of the doorbell. I got up and opened it. It was the policeman. I went and got my notebook and he signed it and left and I went back to my room and turned off the light and lit a cigarette and stretched out on the bed, thinking of my father.

It was night and my father was screaming with pain. I wanted to sleep and so when they took him to the hospital I stayed at home by myself and was happy. When I went to see him, I was shocked by the look in his eyes.

They were wide and anxious and he asked why I'd taken so long. That was as much as he had to say to me. Read to me, he said. I sat on the chair next to him and he rolled over and I picked up a magazine and read to him. After a little while, I leaned over to see his eyes. They were shut. I stopped reading. But then he opened them and said, I'm not done yet, and I read some more. I felt a headache coming on and soon I stopped. He opened his eyes. I went on reading. Finally he said, That's enough, you can go. I left quickly, with a sigh of relief. He didn't ask anything from me after that and I didn't have to see the fear in his eyes. When they brought him home, they carried him from the car to the bed. My brother changed all the seat covers in his place for a darker color, which I didn't understand. When the blood ran out of my father's mouth my brother went downstairs to look for a jar, then returned breathing heavily and said, I looked everywhere. Then he threw himself on the sofa, panting and looking at us. Finally my father lay stiff on his back and they covered his whole body and his face with a white sheet and arranged his limbs in place. They said he didn't ask for me. I lifted the sheet from his face but his eyes were closed.

I slept. In the morning I went to the new apartment my sister was moving into that night. The whole building was new and there was still work being done on some of the floors. The door to the apartment was open. My sister's fiancé was standing in front of it. We both went in, crossing the foyer into the reception room. He showed me a big picture on the wall of a European shore house with a boat in front of it. My brother painted it, he said proudly. Then we went into the bedroom and opened the wardrobe's four drawers. We sat on the bed, bounced up and down, then fingered the blankets and pillows. We went back to the foyer and opened the refrigerator and closed it. He led me to the door and pointed to a lamp above it. If I open the door the light goes on by itself, he said, and it turns itself off when I shut the door. Then he said, Wait for me here while I get the heater and the oven. He left and I sat down in the dark reception room and lit a cigarette. Then I got up and hit the light switch, but the electricity wasn't working yet. I looked at the cover of the lamp above the door. It had the shape of a space satellite. Then I went back and sat at the table and stared at the shiny, unscuffed edges of the chairs. The heater came but not my sister's fiancé. I waited for him some more, smoking, then went to the window. The sun was going down. I saw him walking alone toward the house. He was the only one on the street. Soon he came upstairs and I shook his hand and said, Congratulations. Then I left to go home. I turned on the light and put the notebook in my pocket, sitting on a chair with my back to the door. I picked up a book. Then I got up and turned the seat around to face the door. I went back to my reading. I looked over the edge of the book at the door. The apartment was getting dark. I tried to keep reading but it was no good. I got up and went to the reception room and turned the light on. My neighbor's apartment was dark. I went to the kitchen and turned the light on, then went to my room and picked up the book again. There was a knock at the door. I got up to open it and remembered my sister. She said that when there was a knock at the door she always felt like someone was about to come in and beat her up. So I opened the peephole first and saw the policeman there. I opened up and took the notebook out of my pocket, handing it to him. He signed it and left and I went back to my room. I tried to read again but couldn't. I began pacing. I stopped at the window. All the windows I could see were shut. I took off my clothes and put on my pajamas, then shut the door to my room while leaving the lights on in the reception room and kitchen. I lit a cigarette and stretched out on the bed. When I had smoked it down, I flicked it out the window and turned my face to the wall and slept. I woke up very thirsty, with a headache. I got out of bed. It was still night. I opened the door and went to the bathroom and leaned over the faucet and drank. I turned the water off, but found that the floor of the bathroom was covered with water. I went back to my room. There was a banana on the desk, which I picked up, peeled, and ate, then put the peel on the desk and went back to bed. When I woke up sunlight filled the room. I stayed in bed for a while, then got up and took my toothbrush and soap to the bathroom. The water on the floor had spilled into the reception room. The faucet was broken. I stood in the water and brushed my teeth and washed my face, then went back to my room leaving wet footprints everywhere. I dressed and left the room, shutting its door. I turned off the lights in the living room and the kitchen, then left the apartment and went down to the street. I rode the metro to the last stop and walked along the Corniche. Then I crossed the bridge and went into the first café I found. I chose a table at the back next to the Nile and sat down. A waiter came and I ordered a coffee, then stared at the water. With my eyes, I followed a boat being rowed by a bare-chested young man. One of his oars fell into the water and floated away. He yanked the rudder of the boat and tried to catch the lost oar. He was rowing with just one oar, transferring it from one side of the boat to the other. But the current was against him and as soon as he got close to the oar it floated away. He rowed in a frenzy. Despair showed on his face. Then he threw away his oar and cupped his hands to his mouth and shouted to another rower in a nearby boat, asking for help. But the other rower didn't respond. Maybe he didn't hear. The coffee still hadn't come. I called to the waiter but he wasn't paying attention. I got up and left. I walked to the bridge and caught a bus, getting off at the head of Suleiman Street. I sat down in the first café I saw and drank a coffee, then lit a cigarette. I got up and walked to Tawfiq Street, then down Tawfiqiyya, stopping at Cairo Cinema. It was showing a comedy. I walked toward Fuad Street and crossed it and went down Sharif. I kept walking past Adly and Tharwat in the direction of Suleiman, which I followed all the way to Midan Tahrir. Wastewater covered the ground. The pumps set up everywhere carried water from inside the shops out into the street. The smell was unbearable. I met a man I knew who said he had woken up an hour ago and was rushing to an appointment. I walked fast next to him, saying, I'll go with you to your appointment. But he said that here was where we had to part, and he left me. I crossed the street and headed back in the direction of the Midan. I branched off onto Qasr al-Nil until I reached the cinema. I looked at the posters that said, This is a crazy world. I went to the box office window but the show was sold out. There was a reservations window but the two evening shows were also full. People had booked tickets for tomorrow and the day after. I left the cinema and walked back again to the Midan, then along Suleiman, walking on the opposite side of the street as before. When I arrived at

Cinema Metro, I found it was also showing a comedy. I walked past and stopped at Al Americaine café, not knowing where to go. Cinema Rivoli was on my left, with a huge crowd in front. I remembered the cinemas on Imad al-Din and crossed the street and walked down Fuad to Imad al-Din, where I turned and walked on the left side of the street. There were huge crowds in front of all the cinemas, though they didn't open for another hour and a half. I walked to the end of the street, then went down Ramses toward Bab al-Hadid. It felt like someone was following me. I checked my watch against the station's clock, then headed for a café on the square at the beginning of Gumhuriyya Street, where I sat down in the open air. All at once the sun vanished and everything became gray. I remembered how this neighborhood looked twenty years before, with train smoke rising from Bab al-Hadid and gray colors everywhere. I decided to go look for that old house. Maybe my mother was still there. I got up quickly, before the sun returned. I wanted to approach the house through the fog. I crossed Clot Bey Street, turning off Faggala into the little side streets that connect it with the square. I sensed I was getting close to the house. I was only a few streets away. But I decided to approach it from the direction of Faggala Street, just as my father and I used to do.

We would go by tram, taking it from the Midan just before it turned into Zaher Street. I loved that peaceful street, lined with trees whose branches interlaced overhead in the center of the street, veiling it from the light. And I loved the sound of the trolley pole clearing its path through the branches of the trees. Still, the tram was very fast and we would lift our faces into the afternoon breeze and my father held his tarboosh to make sure it didn't fly off. Then the street ended and the tram turned, swaying a little, into the wide open Midan, slowing its speed and finally stopping in front of the mosque. I would gaze into that big garden, which kept sloping away until it finally disappeared from the view of the tram riders. And through the great stone arches of the mosque wall I would see the red and blue robes of children playing in the garden and keep my eyes on them as the tram slipped back into motion, circling the mosque. Then the mosque and its garden would disappear all at once and my father put his hand on my bare knee while the tram turned sharply past narrow al-Khalig Street and I wished that our tram was the Khalig Street tram so that we could ride between the narrow walls with my father's hand stretched out nearly touching the houses. We would get off at Faggala and my father would take me with his right hand as we crossed the street. We set off down an alley bordered by a high white wall with tree branches swaying over it and the street would grow dark, though the sun was still in the sky, and I understood why when I looked up and saw thick clouds of smoke coming together and then quickly coming apart and my father would say it was the smoke of trains coming from Bab al-Hadid. Then the street ended and the house appeared. My father sat on the bawwab's bench while I went up the long staircase, passing by the doors with their smells of cooking oil. Afterward, my father and I left along the same alley, walking next to the white wall, and I would spot the big bells behind it. The street was hidden in shadows and empty except for us and at the far end a patch of light turned into a tobacconist's shop. We stopped at the entrance, blocked by a big high display case. I pressed my face against the cloudy glass and stared at the boxes of sweets and chocolates. I saw my father's hand dip into his pants pocket. He took out some coins and cast them on top of the glass counter, right at the level of my head, and then we would leave the shop and cross the street to the tram stop. I was

*cold and pressed myself against my father and he spread out the collar of
his jacket to cover his chest and we stood alone on the station platform.
The tram came and we got on the covered back car and huddled in the
corner with my father's warm hand on my bare knee and the tram would
begin the journey back, passing by Khalig Street, then turning abruptly
to the right, the houses on our left disappearing and a dark wide open
space rolling out in front of us. I was afraid that I would fall in and held
onto my father tightly. Then my eyes got used to the dark and I made out
the big Midan with the large form of the mosque in the middle and the
tram would circle the mosque, passing a shuttered cinema that we went
to in the summer with my mother, and then drive down tree-lined Zaher
Street while I leaned my head against the wooden guardrail behind me
and enjoyed the rushing speed, watching my father close his eyes against
the strong wind in our faces.*

I took the tram to the church and turned into the neighbor-
ing street that was crowded and full of noise. The street ended,
I turned to the right. The house I remembered was very high
with wide wooden balconies. My mother jumped from one
of those balconies, landing on the one below. I looked from
house to house. They were all low and only one of them had
wooden balconies. That must be the one, I thought. I walked
slowly toward it. The balconies were small and the lobby
was cramped. The lobby I remembered was spacious. I went
through the lobby and slowly climbed the stairs, coming to
the top sooner than I expected. There was a small room there
and I knocked on the door. Come in, I heard a female voice say.
I pushed open the door and stood in the entrance. There were
three women draped in black sitting cross-legged on a bed in
the corner. One rose and came to me, saying, Who are you? I

recognized my grandmother. I spoke my name in a low voice and she embraced me and kissed me on the cheek. Sit down, she said. I sat on a wooden chair by the door. My grandmother pointed to the younger of the two women. This is your aunt, she said. My aunt rose and kissed me on the cheek. Then she pointed to the other woman. This is my aunt, she said. I rose and picked up my chair and brought it closer to them, setting it down next to the bed. My grandmother's aunt said, This neighborhood is falling apart. My grandmother said, As soon as I saw you, I knew it was you. My aunt said, We were just saying we could meet the two of them on a bus and have no idea. My grandmother picked up the transistor and said, It's story-time. A somber voice on the radio announced another episode of "The Shadow." The episode began with a young man's voice saying tearfully: How can I live when I know my father is a murderer? I sat and listened in silence. All the women gazed at the radio. Fifteen minutes passed, the episode ended, and my grandmother got up to pray. Some children came into the room and my aunt said to them, This is the son of your aunt, may God have mercy on her. She looked at me from the corner of her eye. I said nothing. I wanted to know exactly when and where my mother had died. My grandmother finished her prayers and sat next to me. When exactly did my mother die? I asked her. One week ago tomorrow, she said. Where? At her father's house, she said. I pointed to my head and said, How was she? She read the newspapers and went on about everything better than any of us and she knew what was going to happen and it didn't bother her, my grandmother's aunt said. Then she got sick all of a sudden and wouldn't see the doctor, my grandmother said. She wouldn't take any medicine. She got thinner and thinner and finally stopped eating. My aunt said, On the last day she asked for a cup of water and when she drank it she fell down dead. We were silent. My grandmother said, Even at the end, she didn't want to see me and she didn't want to see any of you. I looked at my watch. The policeman would come soon. I stood up and said, I have to go now. I wished them goodbye. I went downstairs and walked out of the house, then followed some side streets back to Midan Ramses, where I headed for the metro station.

Introduction to the 1986 edition of *That Smell*

The great Yahya Haqqi asked me, when I met him recently at some function or other, whether I remembered his criticism of my first novel, *That Smell*, just after its publication in 1966. When I said yes, he asked my opinion now, almost two decades later, of what he'd said and of my novel more generally. I'd forgotten almost everything to do with the book. Years had passed since the last time I'd read it. I'm not in the habit of going back to previous work—reading like that bores me when it doesn't lead to depression. As for Yahya Haqqi's criticism, I will never forget it.

I'd given the manuscript to a shabby little printer in El Zaher district, during one of those rare moments in the history of modern Egypt when martial law was lifted and a book didn't require prior approval from the censor before being given to a printer. Officially, at least. In fact, the censor kept his office and his job as before. The only difference was that his door no longer had a sign on it, and the confiscation of books didn't happen before the printing, but afterward.

Which is what happened to my novel. The printer had hardly finished before the book was seized. I don't remember if I was summoned to the chief censor's office or if I went there on my own to complain. In any case, I met the late Talat Khalid—one of the more zealous disciples of the Minister of Information, Abdel Qader Hatem—who had called in some departmental bigwigs to enjoy the spectacle. Khalid had a copy of the confiscated novel in front of him, with the margins of most pages marked in red. He asked me, contemptuously, "Why does the hero refuse to sleep with the prostitute his friend brings him? Is the hero impotent?"

I wasn't especially interested in arguing the point. I'd managed to rescue a few of the confiscated copies and began distributing them to writer friends and journalists, asking those with some influence to get the novel released. The late Zaki Murad and I went to see Ahmad Hamrush, then editor-in-chief of *Ruz al-Yusuf*. Hamrush welcomed me very warmly and showed me proofs of the magazine's new issue, which included a short essay by him on my novel titled "The Language of the Age." When I told him about the confiscation he was visibly surprised. He picked up the phone and called his friend Hamdi Hafiz in the Information Bureau; he listened for a moment, and then without replacing the receiver he called the magazine's printer and requested the article be removed.

The news didn't reach most writers and journalists in time, however. A number of magazines and newspapers published reviews, all while the book reposed in the storehouses of the Ministry of Interior.

Yahya Haqqi was one of those to whom I gave a copy of the book. We'd become acquainted a few months earlier, following my release from prison in the middle of 1964. I went to his office at *al-Majalla*, where he was editor-in-chief. He'd opened the magazine's doors to all writers, especially young ones, and would usher them behind the expensive wooden desk at the center of his room, making do with a comfortable leather armchair placed to one side. The first time we met, I brought him my piece on a recent book by Stephen Spender, the British literary critic. I sat and read the article aloud and Haqqi listened intently, studying me with his intelligent eyes and gently correcting my errors of pronunciation. When I'd finished reading, he said he'd take it. It was the first thing I published after my release from prison and I made ten guineas, which covered a month's expenses.

I had gone to see Haqqi with a copy of *That Smell*. He took it from me in a friendly fashion and after reading the title he said, very amiably, that the room was perfumed by the pleasant fragrance emanating from its title.

But it wasn't long before he realized his mistake and wrote a violent review in his weekly column for *al-Masa'*, where he said:

> I am still distressed by this short novel whose reputation has recently become notorious in literary circles. It might have been counted among our best productions had its author not shown such imprudence and lack of good taste. Not content to show us his hero masturbating (if the matter had ended there it would have been of little importance), he also describes the hero's return a day later to where the traces of his sperm lie on the ground. This physiological description absolutely nauseated me, and it prevented me from enjoying the story despite its skillful telling. I am not condemning its morality, but its lack of sensibility, its lowness, its vulgarity. Here is the fault that should have been removed. The reader should have been spared such filth.

So the great writer was asking my opinion of what he called, in his article, my "physiological" style. But while we talked, I began to think about the incident in broader terms. I told him

I felt that I was only now learning how to write. Each new book revealed something new to me about the art, exposing the limits of my abilities, my weak points. And it increased my esteem for those writers who boldly confront the blank page, bristling with the weapons of their craft. This is not at all how I felt when I began writing.

When I wrote *That Smell*, I had just gotten out of prison and was under house arrest, which required me to be at home from dusk to dawn. I spent the rest of the day getting to know the world I'd been away from for more than five years. As soon as I was back in my room, I rushed to record, in quick sketches, all those events and sights that had made an impression on me, that seemed to me completely out of the ordinary. Then I would put the diaries aside and get back to the novel I'd begun in prison, a novel of childhood. I planned for it to consist of a number of independent short stories, connected by the central characters and general theme. I'd finished a few chapters and managed to smuggle them out with the help of my friend Hussein Abd Rabbo, who took them with him upon his own release.

I would turn to the novel but find myself unable to get on with it. I had lost the fire that lit my pen while in prison. The new reality consumed me. And again the familiar question arose: What should I write, how should I write it?

I say "again" because this question was always with me during my time in prison, from the moment I chose to dedicate my life to writing. There were moments I couldn't have cared less about the first half of the question. In the naïveté and enthusiasm of youth, I rebelled against the idea of a necessary relation between form and content in the work of art (a necessity expounded by Mahmoud al-Alim and Abd al-Azeem Anis in their famous articles,* which we were all very excited by in the fifties). Rebellion was the spirit of the age, after all.

The early sixties were a fertile time in politics, in art, in life. It was the moment when a new middle class emerged in Egypt and other countries of the Third World. These countries, benefiting from a favorable balance of global forces, dealt a decisive blow to the old and collapsing colonial order, and fashioned a dream of social justice they weren't able to realize. The socialist movement awoke to the evils of idolatrous individualism and seemed prepared to draw the necessary conclusions. Man had walked on the moon. Sexual behavior went under the microscope, revealing important truths—for example, that a female might naturally enjoy up to fifty orgasms in one night compared to two or three for the average poor male.

From behind the walls of al-Wahat Prison, I and my friends, Kamal al-Qilish, Rauf Mas'ad, and Abdel Hakim Qasim, enthusiastically followed Soviet poets—the young poets Yevtushenko and Voznesensky, as well as the older Tvardovsky—as they exploded conventional forms. We also followed the experiments in spontaneous writing and Op Art in America, and the *nouveau roman* craze in France. Cairene magazines were full of news about literary experiments all over the world. The regime's covert, conservative opposition, which actually controlled publishing and media outlets in the country, cleverly

* See *Fi-l-Thaqafa al-Misriyya* [On Egyptian Culture] (Cairo: Dar al-Fikr al-Jadid, 1955).

promoted the works of Beckett, Ionesco, and Dürrenmatt.

Rebellion was the fuel and experimentalism was the slogan of the day. Naguib Mahfouz put Balzac aside and helped the Arabic novel leapfrog an entire century. New names rose to prominence: Edward Kharrat, Ghalib Halasa, Bahaa Taher, Sulaiman Fayyad, Ibrahim Aslan, Yahya al-Taher Abdallah, and others. I thought I'd found my own path when I discovered Hemingway, by way of two books that managed to breach the walls of al-Wahat. The first was by Carlos Baker and the second was a collection of essays—there was an especially good one by an older Soviet critic whose name I've forgotten—analyzing the great American writer's techniques. I put my faith in these techniques right away (I still do, in certain respects), the most important of which were economy and restraint. Set against the conventionally flabby eloquence of Arabic literature, this "iceberg" style acquired a special sheen. It was under the influence of Hemingway that I began working on my still unfinished novel of childhood.

In the furnished room I rented after my release in the neighborhood of Heliopolis, I would leaf distractedly through the drafts of that novel, asking myself what the point was of writing something that didn't engage the struggle against imperialism, the effort to build socialism, and all the difficulties these efforts brought in their train: terror, torture, prison, death, personal misery.

Then one night I won't forget I glanced over the diary, composed in a telegraphic style, which I wrote in every night after the policeman's departure. There were only a few entries, about sixteen days as I remember. I read the whole thing, then shivered with excitement. There was a buried current running through that telegraphic style, a style that never stopped for self-examination, didn't bother to search for *le mot juste*, nor to make sure that the language was neat and tidy, nor that all ugliness such as might shock delicate sensibilities had been scrubbed away. There was *beauty* in such feeble sentences as: "The writer said that Maupassant said that the artist must create a world that is more beautiful and more simple than our own." And there was a *beauty* in ugly actions, like passing gas in a bourgeois living room.

Wasn't a bit of ugliness necessary to expose an equivalent ugliness in "physiological" acts like beating an unarmed man to death, or shoving a tire pump up his anus, or electric cords into his penis? All because he held a contrary opinion, or defended his freedom and sense of nationalism? Why is it stipulated that we write only about flowers and perfume when shit fills the streets, when sewage water covers the earth and everyone smells it? Or that we only write about creatures seemingly without genitals, so that we don't violate the supposed decency of readers who actually know more about sex than we do?

Reading my brief diaries, I felt that here was the raw material for a work of art. It only needed some arranging and polishing. I felt that I'd finally found my own voice.

I found work at a bookshop selling foreign books (Rauf Mas'ad and Abdel Hakim Qasim later graduated from the same institution). My job required that I man the store all day, so days off were the only time I had for serious writing. I still remember the morning in Ezbekieh Gardens when I wrote the first page of *That Smell*. But I quickly saw that I couldn't go on in this way. I quit work and a friend of mine, Dr. Jamal Saber Gabra, provided me with an unused, book-filled apartment of his in Heliopolis. Surrounded by the writings of archaeologist Sami Gabra (and the tomes of the sainted martyrs), and drawing moral support from my old friends Rauf Mas'ad and Kamal al-Qilish, I worked diligently on my first novel for three months.

I decided to keep the short-winded style that characterized my diaries, though I carefully rearranged their contents, and I used endnotes to clarify a few things. I called the manuscript "The Rotten Smell in My Nose."

Yusuf Idriss, whom I had known since the mid-fifties, opposed the idea of endnotes. He thought they were a bit too innovative and convinced me to move them into the main text. He also argued against the title I'd chosen. In the psychiatric clinic he'd just opened in Midan Giza we came up with "That Smell." He was also kind enough to write an introduction.

Finally, I handed the novel over to a printer, paying him twenty guineas to publish it. The illustrator Mustafa Hussein gave me the design for the cover and Yusuf Idriss's introduction opened the book. There was also a short text on the cover, a kind of manifesto, signed by Kamal al-Qilish, Rauf Mas'ad, and Abdel Hakim Qasim:

> If you do not like the novel now between your hands, the fault isn't ours. It is instead the fault of our cultural moment, dominated as it has been for many years by works of shallowness, naïveté, and conventionalism. To shatter this climate of artistic stagnation, we must turn to the kind of sincere and sometimes agonized writing you find here.

It is in such straits that we introduce this novel by the young writer Sonallah Ibrahim. It will be followed by Nabil Badran's play, "The Blacks," short stories by Kamal al-Qilish, Ahmad Hashem al-Sharif, and Abdel Hakim Qasim, plays by Rauf Mas'ad, and poems by Muhammad Hammam.

These unfamiliar names will introduce an equally unfamiliar art. An art that expresses the spirit of the age and the experience of a generation. An age in which distances and boundaries have vanished, brilliant horizons have opened while dangers threaten, illusions have crumbled and man has penetrated into the truth of existence. A generation born in the shadow of monarchy and feudalism, that went out marching to demand the fall of the King and the British, and that embraced the July Revolution with words and deeds. A generation that has witnessed the collapse of monarchy and capitalism and the construction of socialism—all this in a few short years. A rich and profound experience, full of contradictions and crises, a growing sense of self and knowledge of self. All this requires serious, courageous expression to articulate these experiences creatively and innovatively.

Such is the road we have chosen.

No doubt the reader of today will smile along with me at the tone of absolute self-confidence (reflecting, perhaps, an absolute lack of self-confidence), at those grand phrases, "the truth of existence," and overhasty pronouncements, "the construction of socialism." Such is the naïveté of beginnings, which may also be a form of special pleading.

The days following my novel's publication were hard. At that time, Egyptian newspapers and magazines published nothing but the tired certainties of socialist realism, never neglecting to mention the global play of forces, the technological achievements, etc. (Today these dogmas are parroted by the most backward, reactionary writers, an illustration of their worth and usefulness as ideas.) The Arab nation, with Egypt in the vanguard, was indeed in a dogfight with American imperialism and its Zionist stepdaughter, not to mention Arab conservatives. So it was natural for me to wonder whether I wasn't harming the country by publishing my work under such conditions. Meanwhile, the threat of imprisonment hung over my head.

Many readers took the novel as a butt for jokes and sarcasm. Others exploited it for their own purposes. Abdel Qader Hatem took it to president Gamal Abdel Nasser as proof of the Communists' vulgarity and degeneracy. The Islamic Conference came to the same conclusion. It pained me that my "caper" was used to cast doubt on a movement whose struggles and sacrifices I have honored for many decades. I experienced the same feelings when compelled to publish the novel in 1968 in *Shi'r*, a Beiruti magazine run by Yusuf al-Khal and edited by *al-Nahar* newspaper—neither of which were themselves above suspicion.

But I never regretted writing the novel or publishing it under such circumstances. Nor did I regret the style I wrote it in or ever consider renouncing it. True, I'm often troubled by the sense that I aborted a much greater work. But I'm convinced that such were the limits of my abilities at that time.

Self-criticism, an attention to the interior voice, recognition of the real, an impatience with bourgeois sensitivities and fads—all these continue to be at the basis of my work.

Confiscation didn't put an end to the book for it was already out in the world (a lesson the state apparatuses of Arab countries might learn from). In 1969, while I was abroad, a publishing house called New Culture, once called July Editorial, came out with a second edition of the novel, having removed without my permission everything they imagined might offend the censor. It wouldn't surprise me to learn that the publisher had in fact used a peculiar sort of censor, characteristic of that time, which was the "private editor"—a freelancer who offered his services to authors and publishing houses alike. After an agreement between New Culture and Contemporary Writings, the same edition of the novel was republished in Cairo in 1971.

The current edition is the first complete edition to be published since the initial, confiscated version: the version published by *Shi'r* was not spared the usual scissors, cutting out everything offensive to readers of delicate sensibilities. I have of course corrected the original's errors of syntax and grammar, as well as those of negligence (calling a child "he" in one place and "she" in another, for example). I've also corrected the epigraph by James Joyce. In the original edition I claimed it was taken from *Ulysses* (I'd come across the phrase in the *TLS*, which appears to have misattributed it). When my novel was translated into English by Heinemann in 1971, the translator Denys Johnson-Davies searched that novel long and hard without success. Joyce experts eventually located its source in *Portrait of the Artist as a Young Man*.

SONALLAH IBRAHIM
CAIRO, 1986

NOTES FROM PRISON

All footnotes in this translation are the author's,
from *Yawmiyyat al-Wahat* (2004).

1962

April
Cairo commits suicide. The fire of '52. The city that rose up
and fell destructively on itself. Story of freedom in the streets,
among the people. The great, enormous city from every angle,
its birthing pains.

The hero and the masses—Plekhanov—the cult of personality.

Torture: and since that time he feels that wherever he walks,
whether he's coming in or going out, something will hit him,
something will shock him. If someone surprises him, his
muscles tense. He expects to be slapped or kicked.

June
The thing I seem furthest from, though I think about it all the
time and hope to achieve it, is to deal with man from within.
So many sentiments, so many strange and knotted interior
operations.

Colors and their meanings. Red is love. Yellow jealousy. Blue sadness. Green loyalty. White purity. Purple yearning.

The writer's path is full of sacrifices; everything must submit to his art. Pushkin wasted five years of his life chasing after his girlfriend while she toyed with him. The writer must not allow anything to get in the way of his work or his art. He is a saint and a martyr.

Here is the artist's role in Egypt today. Not to write something enjoyable merely for its aesthetic value. Not simply to lose oneself in philosophical and intellectual issues. Not to live captive to one's individual experience, which could lead to loneliness or to feelings of alienation and absurdity. Not to be content with recording—impressionistically, neutrally, superficially—what happens in society. Instead, the Egyptian artist must work actively and with others. He must dive into the depths of the people and the depths of the individual. He must reveal the way forward, he must choose the direction and change the direction. He must lead and play a role in everyday life, armed with his technique, personal experience, self-awareness, persistence, and the readiness to sacrifice.

The writer is responsible for every word he writes.

"When people talk, listen. Most people don't listen." Advice given by Ernest Hemingway in a letter to a young writer.

"The Beacons," at the Twenty-Second Congress of the Communist Party of the Soviet Union:

—Alexander Tvardovsky: "The hero of my tale, whom I love with all my heart, whom I have tried to depict in all his beauty, who was, is, and will be beautiful, is the truth." Tolstoy.

—"Those writers who hurry to respond to the demands of the day, who apprise us of contemporary events, deserve the sobriquet 'skimmers.' For them, the building of the Volga Canal doesn't merit more than two or three on-the-spot articles, dashed-off and superficial. A mirroring of events and nothing else. But the same subject cost Vladimir Fomenko ten years of hard work. I cannot hide my fear each time I see writers hurrying to spread the news before the events and facts have matured in their minds, before they have experienced a deep need to communicate with the reader."

—Sholokhov: "A writer who speaks of collective farms should know no less than a local agronomist."

—I am a Communist first, a writer after that.

November
"The true material of film is the monologue," Eisenstein.

No real interest in people. Each looks out for himself. Egotism. Where is the spirit of sacrifice, of consciousness-raising?

Psychological problems. Theft. The nature of conditions. Persistent belief in the impossibility of a long-term sentence.

December
The mouth, like the prison, contains, when closed, living things.

A story in two sections: in the first, people enter and do what they do and their actions appear strange, spontaneous, random, futile—in the second section, the same people behaving reasonably, or acting out an interpretation of their previous behavior, or of the laws that governed all those actions that had seemed random, futile, or accidental.

There is a law that governs everything, but we do not know it. Again, the question of coercive conditions, of a power exterior to man. The law of probabilities?

The epic theater of Brecht.

How little I know.

1963

February

One cannot say, with the Surrealists: The world is going to pieces! The question of content is not out of bounds to the artist. We can't keep saying, "There's no longer anything to write about." The conditions in our country do not allow it. A hundred topics await. A hundred horizons open every day.

[...] a negative and dangerous aspect. We will pass through a Stalinist experience. The new generation can't take up politics as a battle of ideas. It's on the verge of becoming a generation of cowards. They've rung down the curtain on the history of revolutionary struggle before the revolution of 1952. [...] The men of the regime are sincere, but they have been schooled in fear. How did revolutionary workers come to hate their country and rejoice at its difficulties?... How have the consciences of so many been destroyed by acts of terror? The humiliation of man. Three months of terror, January–March, 1959.*

*Impressions of Mustafa Sweif's book.***
—Thought Under Pressure (or, the negative aspect of extremist *engagement*). Speaking about what he calls the renunciation of censorship over thought, Freud says some people suffer an inability to set free their spontaneous thoughts. They cannot renounce their critical capacity. This is because desirable thoughts (the artist's thoughts are of this type, since they are essentially libidinal) create a violent resistance, which tries to bar their entry into consciousness. The condition for poetic creation, according to Schiller, is very like what Freud says. In one of his letters to Korner, in which he replies to a friend's complaint about the weakness of his creative powers, Schiller writes, "The reason for your complaint lies, it seems to me, in the constraint which your intellect imposes upon your imagination. Apparently it is not good if the intellect examines too closely the ideas already pouring in at the gates. Regarded in isolation, an idea may be quite insignificant, but it may acquire importance from an idea that follows it; perhaps, in a certain

* The beginning of the paragraph was written in a different pen and carefully erased, apparently out of caution, at the time the papers were taken out of prison. This is the first time criticism of the regime (despite our political support) is frankly expressed. I also erased the words indicated by the ellipses in the middle of the passage.
** Mustafa Sweif was one of the pioneers of psychoanalysis in Arabic. The book referred to here is *The Psychological Bases of Artistic Creativity*, his Master's thesis, published by Dar al-Ma'arif in 1951.

collocation with other ideas, which may seem equally absurd, it may be capable of furnishing a very serviceable link. The intellect cannot judge all these ideas unless it can consider them in connection with these other ideas. In the case of a creative mind, it seems to me, the intellect has withdrawn its watchers from the gates, and the ideas rush in like waves, and only then does it review and inspect the multitude." From Freud's *The Interpretation of Dreams*.

Al-Ahram, February 13, 1963, New Tendencies, "Real Cinema, No Actors, No Scripts, No Studios." Since 1919, some cinéastes have dreamt of a cinema not shot in the studio and requiring no actors. Their idea was basically that the camera should be a tool in the director's hand just as the pen is for the writer. If the writer can rush with his pen to record his reactions to events, why can't the director do the same? Why not take the camera into the street, into the places where people live? If he happens to come across something he'd like to "comment" on, he grabs his camera and records his impression. This is what the Soviet Vertov did, followed by the American Flaherty, and then the two Frenchmen, Epstein and Vigo. Why did they fail to establish a school? Contemporary French cinéaste Jean Rouch says, "The failure stems from a confusion of reportage and drama. They recorded the appearances of life as it is, while the real cinéaste relies on selection. When we carry a camera around and run into something, we put ourselves physically in front of that something. We 'focus' our lens on a particular facet of it, rather than filming the whole. We shut out some elements and concentrate on others. This is obvious from the composition of the shot. After shooting any number of things, we have a film that might take twenty hours to show, from which we select or edit ninety minutes' worth. We 'focus' our idea about the subject, just as a writer prepares his draft for publication." Rouch applies this principle to African societies in Abidjan (Ivory Coast). He was an ethnographer sent to Africa by the French Anthropological Society and based on his experience filming the social life of blacks, he developed a method that made the director the sole author of the film and the reality he recorded its primary subject matter. By selecting from among the elements of struggle in each instance, and by foregrounding that choice by means of montage and cadrage, he transformed the camera into a human eye, one that selects from reality whatever tallies with the director's point of view. In this way, he revealed a new consciousness of reality, one we wouldn't have experienced by looking at things while they were mixed in with the events of ordinary life. Rouch's films—*Chronicle of a Summer*; *Me, a Black Man*; and *The Human Pyramid*—forge a new path for cinema, which critics call "cinema verité," or real cinema. (Zavattini's experience. Cameras in the square, facing the police station.)

May
The Plague, Albert Camus. (Last lines of the novel) "As he listened to the cries of joy that rose above the town, Rieux remembered that this joy was still threatened. He knew from reading his books what the happy crowd did not, which is that the plague bacillus never dies or vanishes for good, that it can sleep for decades in furniture or clothing, that it waits patiently in bedrooms, cellars,

trunks, handkerchiefs, and old papers, and that the day might come when the plague would rouse its rats and send them out among the people, for their immiseration or their instruction, when death would rip them from life's happy embrace."*

Yevtushenko, "Confessions of a Young Soviet," *L'Express*: "The autobiography of a poet is his poetry, everything else is merely a footnote. The poet must offer the reader his feelings, his thoughts, his writings. To deserve the right to speak for others, he must pay the price and submit himself mercilessly to the truth."

—After the Revolution, Soviet poets established the Association of Proletarian Culture and made the decision never to write except in the plural form, to always say "we." At the same time, our literary critics very cleverly devised a theory of "the lyric hero." According to them, the poet was required to extol the loftiest virtues so that he would not appear as himself in his poems, but rather as a model of the perfect man.

—Many old Bolsheviks who were arrested and tortured persisted in believing that they had been abused without Stalin's knowledge. They never accepted that he had personally

---

* I still remember this novel even now when I think about current events. It had a great influence on me despite the poor translation published, I believe, in the "One Thousand Books" series. I also remember my shock at learning that Camus had supported the tripartite aggression against Egypt in 1956.

ordered their treatment. Some of them, after being tortured, traced the words 'Long Live Stalin' in their own blood on the walls of their prison.*

Stravinsky's thoughts on reaching eighty: "Were Eliot and myself merely trying to refit old ships while the other side (Webern, Schoenberg, Joyce, Klee) sought new forms of travel? I believe this interpretation or distinction, much discussed a generation ago, is no longer viable. Our era is but a great unity in which we all share a part. It may indeed seem that Eliot and I made things that lacked living continuity, that we made art out of disjecta membra: quotations from other poets and artists, references to earlier styles ('hints of earlier and other creation'). But we used these things along with anything else that came to hand, treating everything ironically in order to rebuild. We did not pretend to have invented new conveyors or new means of travel, for the true job of the artist is to refit old ships. He can say again, in his way, only what others have already said before him."

In a book he published in '48, entitled *Organon for a Small Theater*, "Brecht rejects his early artistic works as political and didactic. The theater must be a place for aesthetic pleasure and nothing else—though it is also necessary to keep up with the fashions of the age and work scientifically.... We need a theater that does not merely make possible the emotions, in-

* Was I aware, when I copied these lines, of the extent to which they described our own situation at al-Wahat?

sights, and impulses allowed by the relevant field of human relationships in which the actions occur. Instead, we need a theater that will exploit and generate ideas, so that they might play a role in changing the world." *Brecht*, Ronald Gray.

Must write about Cairo after studying her neighborhood by neighborhood, her classes, her evolution.

"You could say that in my last phrase I've joined the new realism. Its characteristic features are not at all the same as those of traditional realism, which is supposed to provide a faithful representation of life. The new realism goes beyond details and rounded characters. This isn't an advance in style, but a change of content. The basis of traditional realism is life—you paint its picture, show how it works, extract its tendencies and what lessons it might offer. That's where the story begins and ends: it depends on life and on the living, the way they dress, the details. For the new realism, the motive for writing lies in ideas, in specific passions that make reality into a means for expressing them." Naguib Mahfouz.

June
John Dos Passos (born 1896), the total, panoramic view. Journalistic spirit. The city itself rather than a particular individual in the *USA Trilogy*.

Hemingway: A tight frame with three dimensions: Simple character. Simple style. Simple setting. In *The Green Hills of Africa*, he talks about four-dimensional prose: the kind that hasn't yet been written, but which is possible. There is a fourth and a fifth dimension (the symbolic?).

Hemingway, The Writer as Artist, Carlos Baker, translated by Dr. Ihsan Abbas.

—On Africa: *"You ought to always write it. Write it down, state what you see and hear, without worrying what you might get out of it."*

—"Where we go, if we are any good, there you can go as we have been." The practical standard is participation. There are other practical standards: the truthfulness of the writing, its vital verisimilitude (in other words, nothing that is in life, whether language, thought, or action, can be wholly excluded without some loss to the vital principle).

—Hemingway's experience in Africa in the translation of reality. He says in the introduction to *Green Hills*: "Given a country as interesting as Africa, a month's hunting there, the determination to tell only the truth, and to make all that into a book—can such a book compete with a work of the imagination?" The answer is that it certainly can, provided the writer is skilled, as well as being committed to both truth and beauty— in other words, the way it was + formal construction. Yet the experiment also proved that the writer who takes no liberties with the events of his experience, who tells things exactly as they were and invents nothing, will place himself at a disadvantage in this competition [the intensity of "The Snows of Kilimanjaro" and "The Life of Francis Macomber"]. This book and the two stories established one aesthetic principle firmly in Hemingway's mind: The highest art must take liberties, not with the truth but with the modes by which truth is translated.

—Hemingway and politics: "A writer can make himself a nice career while he is alive by espousing a political cause, working for it from the inside, making a profession of believing in it, and if it wins he will be very well placed ... But none of this will help him as a writer unless he finds something new to add to human knowledge through his writing."

—*"All bad writers are in love with the epic."*

Eliot to the American poet Donald Hall, in an interview from '59, published in *The Paris Review*: "I think that for me it's been very useful to exercise other activities, such as working in a bank, or publishing even. And I think also that the difficulty of not having as much time as I would like has given me a greater pressure of concentration. I mean it has prevented me from writing too much. The danger, as a rule, of having nothing else to do is that one might write too much rather than concentrating and perfecting smaller amounts."

July

On the night of July 13, '63, I came across the text of a letter I intended to send to my sister. I think constantly of writing to her about my real feelings toward her and of describing many things. But my letters to her travel in more than one direction before they arrive. My sense that someone might read them and smile at their naïveté paralyzes me, as does the thought of meeting someone who had read these letters and could be looking at me and laughing to himself without my knowing. Although actually other people don't care about your sentimentality. The thought that this might be the story of my life.

Is the real problem in art the problem of form? Can we say that the basis of art is form? This doesn't mean we're against content. Form without content is meaningless. (The content of abstract painting is found in the sensations experienced by the self when stimulated by a certain arrangement of colors.) The artist at work is not motivated, in the first place, by a strict idea, but rather by forms and styles. It is by virtue of his working through these forms and styles that the content emerges (the opposite might also occur). In backward societies, or one in which art enjoys a mass audience while it is still culturally backward (Russia at the time of the Revolution), a direct style is necessary and valid.... When the cultural level is higher, when life has become more complex and intellectual development has progressed, the need for more depth—for new forms and styles, for an increasing variety and profundity of each art's creative elements—becomes urgent. (In narrative: memory, experience, symbol, style, scientific awareness.)

If I wanted to describe a picture of my sister when she was young and innocent and wide-eyed and full of possibility—a picture of her wearing a pink skirt with a white spot marking the slight swell of her chest, a trace of sweat above her shoulders—can words succeed in describing her, in translating the feeling that digs into my chest? Film can do it better. So another way must be sought, beyond the snapshot, to capture this feeling in words.

August

The mood in the prison has become unbearable. Terrible noise. I can't sleep at night or in the afternoon. I wish the prisoners were gone. I don't know how to work; I'm constantly depressed and nothing changes my mood except reading a good story or something about the writer's craft. I'm confident I know how to write, but what nearly destroys me is not knowing the level of writer I'll become. Many thoughts run through my head, which I want to express but can't. I don't know how to express my thoughts clearly in speech. If I try to write them down, the thoughts run away.

When we express ourselves, we also express the collective. A fence gleaning.* What is shared by these collectives: boredom,

---

* I had the habit of going after lunch to the remotest spot in the prison's courtyard, right up against the outer fence, to escape the noise of the cells and to have a short siesta. I took a blanket with me and spread it over the sands, and a towel to cover my face and protect it from flies. When I woke up, I would go to the cells for some tea and take it back with me to the fence. I drank it out of a yellow plastic cup, which I kept clean by washing it regularly with sand. My sister sent me provisions of Republic-brand tea and since leaving prison I have never found anything like it in any of the many places I have traveled. There, by the fence, sometimes refreshed by a humid breeze that would lift the summer heat, I was able to concentrate and write several short stories.

disgust, disillusionment. The romanticism of struggle is over. What remains are the utterly naked facts. The cult of personality and its collapse. Rethinking of everything. The masks are off (the mask of religion, the mask of heroism …).

Eye of the child: "Human nature seeks constantly to know the world around it, but the desire decreases over time. As we grow older the world loses its beauty and brilliance, but we can reclaim our acuity of vision, the sunrise of the world, by way of the child who observes the world around him with wide and curious eyes."

September
September 2, afternoon: I dreamed of my father. He was walking and he put his arm around my shoulder and embraced me. He seemed strong, solid. He complained to me about the troubles and pains of last year. I told him that as for myself, I'd been in pain since turning eighteen. It made me happy to complain to him and expect some kind of relief. But he pointed to the crowded tram and said, smiling kindly, "They're going to pick each other's pockets," and I realized he wanted to change the subject. Then he disappeared and Adel H. took his place.* We walked next to each other with his arm on my shoulder and I began to complain to him, too. He sympathized, then left me when we reached a playing field. I was angry, because he had listened to me only so that I'd accompany him to the play-

---

* Adel H. was Adel Hussein—later Vice President of the Work Party— who was one of the prisoners at al-Wahat and once shared a cell with me.

ing field, not because he was especially interested in what I was saying. I went away, after taking his towel in revenge. I woke up and felt happy about seeing my father. I recalled my feelings of delight, gladness, comfort at being able to complain to him and have his help. I thought, if only there were no science of dreams. How wonderful it would have been if this were a visit from my father's spirit—a consolation, a prophecy!

Read an article, "The Dialectic of Nature." Planets in motion, the earth cooling, establishing the conditions of life, the first cell, the vertebrates, mankind, mankind in its most advanced stage, the extinction of the earth (its cooling, its collapse into the sun), the persistence of matter in alternate forms in an infinite universe. Subject for a great novel.

Virginia Woolf's *To The Lighthouse* has opened up a new world for me.... Her idea of art seems to be the same as that given in her novel by the painter: "One wanted, she thought, dipping her brush deliberately, to be on a level with ordinary experience, to feel simply that's a chair, that's a table, and yet at the same time, It's a miracle, it's an ecstasy." This is what Woolf does in the novel, handling everything that is simple, ordinary, quotidian. She writes by magic, elegantly and simply, without artifice: "But he did not ask them anything. He sat and looked at the island and he might be thinking, We perished, each alone, or he might be thinking, I have reached it. I have found it; but he said nothing."

Anything that takes us beyond the limits of the conventional novel, now exhausted, is worth doing. I believe writing, the practice itself, will reveal the ingredients of experimentation, will be the incarnation of its content.

How shall I write? I don't think I have to write about any given topic—that is, sit down to write it and find a suitable form. Not at all. My feelings are set in motion by an idea, an experience, a memory, a style, a form, and they demand release. In releasing them, they interact with my rational mind, which determines their form and content.

Depths of the sea: a book by William Beebe, *A Half Mile Down*—"At a depth of eighteen meters, red light vanishes. Yellow vanishes at one hundred. Two hundred and forty meters down, green and blue also vanish from the spectrum, giving way to a deep blackish blue. Between 520 and 580 meters, we were enclosed in utter blackness." A battle in the deep dark waters between a whale … and a nine-meter squid. With its snaky, suckered tentacles it measures 15 meters. A strange world, where darkness reigns, unsafe, unchanging, ice-cold, almost without oxygen. But there is life. About the Japanese shrimp, Dr. Noginama says that the act of insemination occurs between midnight and eight in the morning on mild and calm summer nights, in fresh water: "The male pursues the female … gripping her as she tries to flee him … and tears off her outer shell. He then embraces the naked female and she takes his organ of reproduction, brutally and coarsely, inside her, then rips it off ... so that he remains in a state of impotency until a new organ takes the place of the old."

The rest of Yevtushenko's article in *L'Express*:

—Prose is far less tractable than poetry. A novel can't be written in a few days, nor read aloud to the public.

—Realism is the greatest *ism* of art. But realism, as I understand it, can assume hundreds if not thousands of different forms. ... Each work that moves the spirit of man, whether or not it represents houses, people, and trees, I take to be a work of realism.

—Once a tired woman worker came up to me and said, "Just write the truth, son, just the truth. ... Look for the truth in yourself and take it to the people. Look for the truth in the people and store it within yourself."

November
Eliot's "objective correlative": he means an image through which the poet articulates his emotion, so that the image provokes a similar emotion in the reader. This emotion is not a feeling but rather the transformation of feeling into an image, for poetry is not an expression of feelings but rather an escape from them. It is the poet's effort to transform his personal pains into something strange and fertile, something universal that accords with a general rather than selfish interest.

Can I unify the personal with the objective in my writing? Set off in three directions at the same time: subject, style, and form.

My father taught me to put no store in anything whose only justification was custom. I learned from him that I must think about everything for myself, on my own terms.

Naguib Mahfouz's style in *The Search* is the same style I used last year in my own writing. It's also derived from Joyce and Woolf. Mahfouz's novel, of which only four parts have so far appeared, will be the beginning of the modern Egyptian novel.

December
"I projected *The Battleship Potemkin* as a consecutive series of events, a dramatic totality. The secret of the work's unity lies in my having arranged the events according to the laws of tragedy, a classical tragedy in five acts. I divided the events of the film into five acts and in each act treated specific events, whose meaning was dependent on the events that preceded and followed them, with the stipulation that each shot add something new to what came before.... Each shot has a particular meaning and the general idea of the film does not lie in the film itself, but is rather created by the spectator through his tracking of the events, which were selected from among the facts of the historical narrative." "A Director's Thoughts," Sergei Eisenstein.

Friday, December 20, 1963. How wonderful suddenly to hear a word of praise directed at something of yours which no one else found value in. A. said something that's turned my head; I don't know what to say or to think. It's a beautiful thing to have someone call you a kind of genius, or to say that you will make something truly new. But is it true? I've been searching for the new, which is why I was so irritated to discover Naguib Mahfouz using stream-of-consciousness in *The Search*, just as I had....Well then, will I repeat him? ... Must look for something new.... I have just realized that stream-of-consciousness, in the novel and in the short story, is on the march all over the world, including Egypt. And I've become irritated by all those ready-made phrases, now turned into fossils: He walked, he went, he said. Can our country innovate in the novel on a world scale?

A.'s words to the effect that man had discovered the scientific method and used it in his life, and that the method must be reflected in his literature.

Realism in art and literature was a new vision of the world following the transformation of material, social, and political conditions in the eighteenth and nineteenth centuries, specifically the industrial revolution. The writer no longer wrote to save mankind from its boredom, nor to help them pass the time. He aimed his discoveries at the darkness surrounding his field of vision. He was enriched by new movements in morality and politics, which left their marks on literary and artistic groups: partisan literature and realism → psychological realism, historical realism, social realism, materialist realism, socialist realism, revolutionary realism.

All these schools represented a persistent attempt to reach reality, as well as a quest for new forms. Surrealism was not a mode of pessimism nor escapism, as frivolous people suppose. It was another attempt, motivated by the nightmare of World War I, to discover reality, which had abruptly demonstrated the impotence of previous schools to articulate and uncover it. Socialist realism played this same role in the age of science. But it failed due to intellectual stagnation, Leftism, and an "unscientific" approach to reality (its neglect of contradictions, its gaudy picture-painting, and its commitment to a style and technique that were out-of-date). Scientific socialism is a science, not a method. There is no commitment. There is only the issue of the scientific method.... Art is opposed to daily politics. It takes a long, comprehensive view. Trial and error. It is not a tool, but open to all newness. Lenin and the freedom of the imagination.

Life will have no meaning unless we stop at once and look at it and see all the things we have been blind to ... unless we look at everything that lies below the surface, unless our curiosity is fired by the miracle of the everyday.

Toward a new movement in the novel and the short story. Why is there a crisis? We don't have a long history in this art form. Our reality has changed in bewildering fashion; it's no longer possible to represent this reality using the old methods.

The development of this art form cannot happen in Egypt as it happened in Europe. We need a true leap forward.

"The directors of the New Wave face up to the absence of conventional drama. They put characters on display, but do not attempt to have them make sense. Their films are entirely free of the structure of conventional drama. So long as the camera is no longer constrained to tell a continuous story with beginning, middle, and end, it can represent what it sees, just as in life. For life is not orderly, its unity is incomprehensible, its one continuity is its principle character, the axis of life and its events." Alexandre Astruc in *Le Monde*, August 12, 1959.

"Why Neorealism Failed," Eric Rhode, translated by Ata' al-Naqqash for *al-Katib*, April 1963: Moravia believes neorealism ended because it fulfilled its task, which was "to respond to the pressing need, after the war, to account for every kind of deficiency brought about by defeat and national disaster." Neorealism offered more than merely spiritual succor. It was an attempt once again to go back to the beginning: What is man? What are his rights and responsibilities?

— "The reality buried under myths flowered once again. Cinema remade the world. Here was a tree, an old man, a house, a man eating, a man sleeping, a man screaming." Cesar Zavattini.

—Principles of the movement:
1) An end to naïve clichés.
2) An end to imaginary and grotesque fabrications.

3) An end to historical narratives and the adaptations of novels and stories into films.

4) An end to the rhetoric that represented Italians in general as on fire with the same noble sentiments ... making all of them equally aware of all the problems of life.

—Zola defined the naturalist writer: "His great concern is to gather material and to find out what he can do in this world he wishes to describe. When this material is collected, the novel will spontaneously find its form. The writer has only to gather the facts and put them into a realistic frame. The oddities of the story must not claim his attention. On the contrary, the more the narrative is shared and universal, the better...."

—*Umberto D* is the closest Zavattini has come to his ideal of inserting 90 consecutive minutes from the life of man into a film.... Here we are confronted with a paradox of neorealist film, which presents, at moments, a reality broken off from life and therefore as meaningless as the realism of Alain Robbe-Grillet's *Le Voyeur*. But this should not surprise us, because it is the logical development of Zola's idea of collecting the facts and then seeing what significance or importance they bear in and of themselves.

—Georg Lukacs says of Zola: "Perhaps no one has been able to paint so precisely and suggestively the exterior trappings of modern life. But merely the exterior trappings.... These constitute the enormous backdrop in front of which minuscule people come and go, acting out with random gestures their accidental lives. Zola was unable to discern what the great realists such as Balzac, Tolstoy, or Dickens, had achieved by representing social institutions as human relations, and social phenomena as composed of these relations...."

—Description and analysis is substituted for epic situations and plots.

For realism, as for Aristotle, the characteristic procedure of art is its method of imitating an action.

Writers at Work: The Paris Review Interviews, Van Wyck Brooks (Viking).

— "I believe that it is no longer possible for lyric poetry to express the immensity of our experience. Life has grown too cumbersome, too complicated." Pasternak.

—"I always feel it's not wise to violate rules until you know how to observe them." Eliot.

On Le Nouveau Roman

—"Only through writing can the writer uncover new artistic values." Alain Robbe-Grillet.

—"The writer must distance himself from visible, known, and studied reality. He must focus on the interior world that is strange to him." Nathalie Sarraute.

"He would write a book when he got through with this. But only about the things he knew, truly, and about what he knew. I will have to be a much better writer than I am now to handle them he thought. The things he had come to know in this war were not so simple." Hemingway, *For Whom the Bell Tolls*.

1964

January

Naguib Mahfouz in *al-Katib*: "When the novel was interested in life as such, the traditional style was the most appropriate. Human character appeared in all its details. When life becomes a problem, the human being cannot be a particular person but simply a human being.... Details vanish, along with narrative, and dialogue dominates all the other aspects.... When man stands face-to-face with his destiny, details lose their value."

The only essential commitment of art is to the truth.

Sex and Morality in the United States, *Time Magazine*:

—Hemingway's phrase has become a moral law: "What is moral is what you feel good after, and what is immoral is what you feel bad after."

—It is part and symptom of an era in which morals are deemed private and relative. Pleasure is more like a constitutional right than a privilege, and self-denial is increasingly seen as foolish rather than virtuous.

—The days of its bold talk of sexual freedom long over, Communism has now become the most powerful force for Puritanism in the world.

—Radcliffe girls believe that necking is dirty because it provokes desire without satisfying it. Intercourse is therefore more virtuous.

—The new sexual freedom in the United States does not necessarily set people free.... The great new sin today is no longer giving in to desire, but not giving into it fully and successfully. While enjoyment of sex has increased for many, the competitive mania to prove oneself as a functioning sexual machine makes many others feel neurotically guilty, and therefore impotent or sexually frigid.

Sartre's article on the Soviet film *Ivan's Childhood*, in *Les Lettres Françaises*, the literary magazine of the French Communist Party: "The better socialist realist productions have, in spite of everything, always given us complex, nuanced heroes; they have exalted their merits while taking care to underline certain of their weaknesses. In truth, the problem is not one of measuring out the vices and virtues of the hero but one of putting heroism itself into discussion. Not to deny it but to understand it."

March

March 7, I've been trying for two days to start writing again. I thought I had figured out what it was really about and how I would write it. But when I start writing I become frightened. Early yesterday I cried because I couldn't go on for more than two pages. I felt like I'd lost something. I hadn't thought I would write at night, but then I felt a strong urge and had a clear mind—but with the same result.

"… I read it and was really upset, because it taught me the story of mom and dad, and you and me. It taught me how much effort it cost dad before he could take me away from my mother, and how much worry we caused him. He could have lived in a nice place if we had never existed. But thank God he did keep at it until he could take me away from my mother's family. I would have been so miserable if I lived with her. It also taught me what Mama Aisha did to us, and a lot of other stuff I hadn't known before. You're the one who knows everything. I liked the story because you took it from real life. I mean there's not too much fantasy in it. I also liked your style and your way of putting things. It's not the normal way. There's something a little strange about it and this was the best thing in your story—your way of putting things. But how did you remember everything so exactly?

"I hope you'll forget the bad stuff, especially about Mama Aisha. She's changed a lot, to the point where now you can't believe the bad things she did. She's the one who insisted on visiting you in Qanatir prison, both times, and she always asks about you. So I hope you'll forget the rest. As for everything else…." From my sister's letter.

The flash-forward, to which Raauf has assigned great importance: It is one element in our new vision of reality. An example from Port Saeed: A. R. is fighting courageously and at the same time we cut to see him ten years later in different conditions. Another example, from the correction of man in prison: the torture reaches a certain level, then stops; five years later, in an ordinary setting, he talks forcibly, calmly, confidently, and from a place of power; but if the torture had been one tick more severe, his fate would have been completely different. In a tragedy of Djamila Bouhired, she is re-imprisoned after liberation. Knowledge of this at the beginning lends strength.*

---

* It seems that Raauf Mas'ad, one of our group, wrote a play in which he used the technique of what he called "a leap into the future" (the opposite of a flashback). This naïve idea sprang from a desire to prove ourselves and create "a new vision"—thereby ignoring, or pretending to ignore the fact that the English writer J. B. Priestley had already represented his characters as meeting multiple fates.

"A. R." is probably Ahmad Rufa'i, a leader of the Communist Party and the popular clandestine resistance to the British in Port Saeed. Along with Abdel Mun'am Shatila and Sa'ad Rahmi, and with the cooperation of several Free Officers in the entourage of Abdel Nasser, he was able to smuggle arms into the city by way of Lake Manzala. Resistance operations inside Port Saeed, culminating in a massive demonstration, threatened the British position. None of this prevented Rufa'i's arrest and conviction in January 1959. He remained in prison until he was released in the general amnesty of mid-1964.

From *Nouvelle Critique*, December 1962, Claude Prévost. "The Battle for Moscow, sixteen years after," on Aleksandr Bek's two novels *Volokolamsk Highway*, published in 1944, and *Several Days*, published in 1960.

—If the critic's theory of "an absence of conflict" did harm to the theater, it also harmed the novel, pushing it to refuse a treatment of detail, which critics supposed would lead to naturalism.... (Realism is the organization of detail, which must not be neglected or bypassed, but rather clarified in general. To neglect details, with the excuse that they are sordid, is anti-realist. In war, this neglect becomes a betrayal of realism, for the basis of war is sordidness.)

April
April 3, shots. The wounding of Louis Ishaq,* then his death. Peace of mind?

April 9, silent funereal. Afternoon at the gate: a wonderful wind, with the garden in front of us. The disc of the sun behind

---

* The release of prisoners finally began in small groups. At the same time, there were persistent efforts to stop or delay this operation. April third was set as a day for the release of a few prisoners and their friends and acquaintances gathered at the prison gate to say goodbye. Suddenly an officer named Subhi, who had just arrived in the prison, began acting wildly and started a fight. He had already alerted the wall sentries and given them the order to fire at any sign of trouble. They did indeed shoot, at random, and they hit Louis Ishaq, one of the most prominent Communist leaders.

the mountains, a big, perfect, yellow-orange circle, surrounded by gray (those who criticize abstraction are asses).

I am reading Freud. What he says about sexual symbols is important. The airplane.

On dreams: <u>condensation</u>: the coherence of parts and elements that have no connection to each other in reality, as in the paintings of Böcklin—the bells—the visual image (via retrospective translation).